Echo of a Dream

A sequel to Elusive Dream

by

Ella Sailor

PUBLISH AMERICA

PublishAmerica
Baltimore

To Jo-Ann

my special friend

my pride and joy

my daughter

Grateful Acknowledgement

I gratefully acknowledge the time and energy my son, Gerry, spent in reviewing the manuscript and lending his expertise—"Really, Mother, do lawyers still drive big Oldsmobiles?" Thank you, Ger, for your support, and for cheering me on.

And special thanks to my husband, Jack, for your love, encouragement, and for being there when I need you most.

CHAPTER ONE

He eased the sleek BMW in behind her small grey Honda and quietly opened the door. He thought he might find her here. The hospital said she had been discharged several hours earlier.

Sobbing uncontrollably, she knelt by the tiny grave. She noted the temporary marker...a small white cross...*Merri-Lee Walker*. So he had named their baby!

He longed to take her in his arms–they should be grieving together–but he had forfeited his right. He could scarce watch as her tears spilled unrestrained onto the small mound.

At length she retrieved a hand spade from her bag. Removing the withered cut flowers, she dug into the soft earth, and carefully planted the miniature rose–its pink buds and blossoms speaking of life. She watered it slowly from her water bottle, watching the earth moisten.

Then lifting her hands, palms up, she whispered a prayer as though surrendering her baby into the hands of the Almighty.

She rose quickly...pausing only a moment by her parents' graves before turning away. If she saw the grieving father waiting, she gave no indication. Nor was his presence acknowledged as he hurried to open her car door.

The starter argued once...twice...three times; the vehicle coughed into life and complained its way toward the gate. He berated himself. How many times had she mentioned the problem? Always he assured her he would take care of it.

Now following at a distance, he waited while she parked in the double garage; he watched the automatic door close slowly behind her.

He would return to the office–let her get a good rest–then leave early and pick up her favourite Chinese food. It had been a long time since they'd eaten together in front of the fireplace–it had been a long time since they had eaten together!

By 4:30 he was home. Noting with satisfaction that the Honda was still there, he parked beside it, then moved quietly, putting the food to warm while he set a small table near the fireplace.

"Lee," he called softly as he tapped on the bedroom door. "Supper's ready, Kitten." Carefully he opened the door, repeating her name over and over. The bed had not been slept in...the bathroom–vacant...the closet door–ajar. Slowly...it dawned on him...her closet was empty...she was gone!

The cold, familiar numbness took over his mind and emotions–the same numbness he had experienced for most of the past four months...while she had been ill. He fought to keep control.

He wished he could have done it differently...not moved into the guest room...not put in fifteen-hour days at the office...the library. If only he had come when she needed him...when she needed the doctor, he agonized.

He wandered aimlessly from room to room. Her personal things were definitely gone. How could she have packed? She was so weak...so sick...for so-o long. She must have had help. Maybe her sister-in-law, Sherry. Well, he would just give her a call.

"Sherry, it's Brett. Do you know where Leanne is?" His voice was abrupt, to the point.

"No, no, I haven't seen her. Isn't she still in the hospital?"

"She was discharged this morning. I saw her at the cemetery...followed her home. Her car is still here, but she's gone."

"She wouldn't go far with *that* car!" He flinched as she continued, "It wouldn't get her to the end of the block, but she could be shopping...visiting. Have you called Aunt Maude?"

"No...no! She's gone...her things are all gone. You don't know anything about this?" His tone was bordering on accusatory.

"No, Brett. She didn't mention anything to us; we didn't know she was getting out today."

He wandered again through the lifeless rooms...the master bedroom where they had laughed and loved for the first fourteen months of their marriage.... His gaze took in their wedding picture– the radiant bride, her dark hair piled high around her crown...her eyes glowing with love...looking into his. It mocked him now. He turned away. Her jewelled ring box stood on the dresser. He flicked the lid. The diamonds, too, mocked him. She had left them behind. He stood...holding the box...running his fingers over the rich jewels inside and out. He wanted to throw it at the wall...then after a few moments, he carefully replaced it on the dresser..

Well...she was his wife...rings or no rings...and he would find her.

His troubled thoughts were interrupted by a light tap on the door. He didn't want to see anyone...not now...not ever. His world had collapsed.

"Brett, it's Dave," his brother-in-law let himself in through the unlocked door. "Brett, what's going on? Sherry says that Lee...." He stopped at the stricken look, the tear-stained face and hurried to put an arm around his shoulders. Brett was not only his brother-in-law, but his good friend...his partner in law practice. "Heh, Buddy, we'll work on this together. What do you think happened? Do you know where she'd go?"

The distraught husband ran his hands through dishevelled sandy hair, then shrugged his shoulders as if afraid to trust his voice.

Dave noted the small table set in front of the fireplace, smelled the Chinese food. A quiet, intimate evening had obviously been planned...at least by Brett.

"Have you checked with the hospital? The neighbours? Aunt Maude?"

Again he shook his head...obviously in shock, the brother-in-law decided.

"Shall I call around?"

"No...please. I just need some time...I can't think right now."

"Brett, you need to eat something. Let's get you some of what

I'm getting a whiff of."

He shook his head, "Don't think I can."

"We'd better give it a try, fella'. Have you eaten today? Stress is a killer!" He opened the small cartons with the steaming food and insisted they eat together. They were both surprised when Brett ate a small portion.

"Do you think she's all right?" he asked at length.

"Leanne? Of course she is. You know her. She will have her plans all laid out. Guess I'm wondering what would make her do such a thing."

"Me."

"Why do you say that?"

"Guess I've been pretty numb for the past four months or so...since she got so sick...I just haven't been there for her...don't quite know how it happened...why it happened...." his voice broke.

"I don't quite understand. Lee hasn't said anything to us. We knew she was sick...."

"Don't think any of us knew how sick. She's not one to complain, but it grieves me to remember that she asked for my help a few times and I...I...."

"Easy, Buddy; take it easy. Don't go there! Guilt can eat you alive. Do you think she may have gone to the condo in Toronto?"

"I wondered about that but it's rented out right now, at least till the end of the term."

"Well, she obviously had a plan in mind–she had to have somewhere to move her personal stuff. Computer gone?"

"Yeah. Most everything she'll need. She left her furniture...her mom's dining room suite...fancy dishes and stuff."

"She must have made some arrangements by phone. Maybe we'll just call the phone company and get a list of calls for this month. Have you tried calling her cell?" he added

Brett shook his head. "If she's hiding, she won't be answering. Actually, we just got a phone bill; haven't even looked at it. Lee usually paid the bills."

"It certainly seems that Toronto figured big on her mind if this is an indicator," Dave suggested. "Do you recognize any of these numbers?"

"Just the condo," Brett replied. "Oh, yeah, I think that's the University of Toronto, probably the Dean's office. Most of these were third-number calls. She must have made them from the hospital...looks like they were made almost a month ago...."

"That must have been when she was in for that blood transfusion."

Brett's face was a study in confusion and self incrimination. "Oh, God," he murmured. "Oh, God."

"We better find out what's going on," her brother continued. "Let's check the locals first."

"Modern Moving and Storage," a pleasant female voice responded.

"Guess we know how she moved," he looked at Brett. "Now to find out where."

Suddenly Brett couldn't go on. "No, Dave, no." His grief seemed too deep, too personal to share–even with his wife's brother. "Let me sleep on this and maybe tomorrow...." He couldn't let Dave know that some of those repeated calls had been to a number he recognized only too well.

CHAPTER TWO

He knew he should go for a run...a walk...work out...do something to get rid of the overwhelming stress that disabled him. Sleep would be in short supply and tomorrow would be a full day in court. If only he could satisfy himself that the repeated phone numbers had really not been Bill's after all. He couldn't bring himself to check the phone book...call...or ? Could the truth really be worse than the endless guessing? "Oh, God," he prayed, "I need your wisdom."

First, he would run, lack of strength not withstanding. Numbing-out was no longer an option–it had gotten him into this mess!

He returned an hour later; his adrenalin finally at a manageable level. He would leave the phone calls for a few days...at least until this trial was over...then he would find Leanne–Bill or no Bill.

It had been a long and brutal week, but the outcome in court had been positive. He knew it was by God's grace that he had been able to keep his wits about him.

His mid-week phone call to the Toronto number had confirmed his worst fear. The recorded message had informed him that he had reached Bill's Interior Decorating and Design, and invited him to leave a message. So...she had called Bill when she was in distress. *She called me first,* he berated himself, *and I didn't respond. It seems Bill was there when she needed him.*

Now it was Friday afternoon and he was on his way to Toronto. First he had an important appointment...too important to be ignored...then he would call on Bill.

He thought he had prepared well enough to encounter Bill, but now as he rang the doorbell he found himself whispering a prayer.

The warm smile of the shapely redhead disarmed him. "You're in luck; he just arrived. I didn't realize he had another appointment today," she commented as she showed him into Bill's office and private sanctuary.

The man behind the desk was much smaller than he had expected–probably about five ten, he estimated. His thick brown hair curled about his ears and–together with the gold stud in his ear–gave him the appearance of youth. The office was decorated in warm pastels designed to bring out a soft glow in the light oak furnishings. Prints of lavishly decorated interiors covered the walls, and swatches of materials and draperies filled a wall of shelves.

Bill looked up from his computer in surprise as Brett introduced himself.

"I'm sorry to interrupt your deliberations," he began, "but I'm Brett Walker and I'm wondering if you might have been in contact with Leanne."

"Mr. Walker...Brett...I am glad to meet you.," he rose extending his hand. "Yes...yes...we are friends of Leanne. She spent the week with us...recuperating. May I offer our condolences for your grief."

"Thank you," Brett replied curtly. "And Leanne?"

"I took her to the airport this morning."

"Airport?"

"Yes. Yes. She was flying to Heathrow...England...you know...to attend her cousin's wedding. I believe she plans to stay a few weeks," he added quickly.

Brett found himself floundering momentarily, then asked, "So she spent the week here with you?"

"Yes...yes, she did. She and my wife Billie are great friends. Actually she introduced me to Billie. You would have met her when you came in? Can you join us for dinner? You must meet our wee Willie."

Brett was both embarrassed and relieved. Things were not as bad as he had imagined...he found himself liking Bill. He could easily see how his friendship had appealed to Lee. Perhaps he should stay for dinner and let them tell him what they knew of her plans.

"I'm sorry I don't mean to intrude on your quiet evening at home," he began, "but I am concerned for Lee. I'm afraid we've been through a terrible time these last months, and Lee has borne the brunt...."

"Yes...yes, we're aware, but I assure you we would love to have you join us for the evening meal...if you have no other plans."

"Thank you, I appreciate your kindness," he replied, feeling slightly more comfortable.

"May I hold her?" he asked as they enjoyed tea. Billie handed over the delightful three-month old Wilhelmina, with a warm smile. He held her close, looking into her huge blue eyes and running his thumb down her little cherub cheeks. "Willie really suits her," he said, gently kissing the top of her head and noting it was already covered with soft red fuzz. "She's beautiful...like her mamma," he offered, then looked down quickly lest they see the tears.

It had been only weeks since he held his own tiny one–so very tiny–and kissed the soft little head covered with dark fuzz. She was beautiful, too, like her mamma except for the bruises inflicted by the efforts to save her life. But her mamma had never seen her. She died in his arms and was buried before Lee regained consciousness.

Sensing his unspoken pain, Billie asked, "Can you tell us about your little one, Brett? Lee really didn't know much...."

He nodded. "Lee didn't regain consciousness until a few days after the funeral. I guess you know that she'd been sick through most of her pregnancy, lost a lot of weight. Doctors couldn't seem to get to the bottom of the problem. It started soon after conception. She always said something didn't seem right; she didn't want to get pregnant until she found out she was okay. The obstetrician assured us she was just fine and was simply a reluctant mom. I'm sure she gave in because she knew how badly I wanted a child. Then," he paused, realizing he was rattling on, "they wanted her to abort when they thought the child may have brain damage. She refused, of course. She was ready to give her life for the little one...and very nearly did. The baby was a month premature and...." he broke off, unable to go on. He couldn't tell them how she had called his office when she needed to go to the hospital. He hadn't bothered to pick it up, then suddenly was seized with an urgency to get home. He arrived as the ambulance was pulling away and followed it to the hospital–she was already unconscious.

"Tell me about Lee," he changed the subject.

"She was doing pretty well, all things considered," Billie began. "Of course she was very pale, thin, not very strong. I tried to persuade her not to go to England; I wanted her to stay with us a few weeks and let me care for her. She cared for me, you know, for more than a month when I was in University; I had pneumonia with complications and nowhere to go. But she wouldn't stay with us now; she wanted to get to England. I know her aunt will see that she's well cared for; she's a celiac, too, and will know how to help her. They seem to be quite close."

The gifted litigator opened his mouth as if to reply, then nodded mutely. So they had discovered celiac disease...he wondered how long she'd known. He would have to find out about it and if it could be fatal.

"I was able to help her some...with her diet, I mean. I guess you know I'm a nurse," she went on, "and I have a friend who's a dietician. We put some things together for her that would be easy...she's way too weak to cook for herself."

"Thank you," he said, "thank you for caring for her." Then allowing his curiosity and concern to outweigh his pride, he ventured, "Can you tell me about this disease ...celiac?"

She nodded. "Celiac is an allergy to gluten...found in wheat, but also in a number of other grains. It disables the small intestine by destroying the small digestive hairs. Since the small intestine is our main digestive organ, the body suffers from malnutrition. Leanne's body and that of the little one were depleted. I guess you know that's why the doctors feared brain damage...and wanted her to abort...."

"I guess I don't understand why the brain damage."

"She couldn't absorb iron, the blood was constantly low in haemoglobin...that's the oxygen carrier...that's why she had so many blood transfusions...." She stopped at the look of anguish as his tears ran unchecked. He couldn't bring himself to tell them that he knew of only one transfusion.

Why have I ignored her all these months? he asked himself over and over again. *O God, help me to find out what's wrong with me, so I can make it right.*

"Do you know what her plans are?" he asked, trying to compose himself.

"She plans to stay in England for a few weeks...perhaps a month or more...depending on how well she comes along."

"And after that?"

"I believe she plans to pursue her masters degree...she said something about the university allowing her the scholarship. I had offered to look after the baby since I would be at home anyway... knowing that she might need extra help...you know...." she gestured with her hands, noting his confusion, "since I'm a pediatric nurse...."

His mind whirled, trying to make sense of the information. *So...she was going to leave me even if the baby lived. Why didn't she tell me?* He cringed inside, realizing she had asked for his input...she'd had to make a decision regarding the baby's birth...where it would be born...whether he would assist her. He cringed again as he remembered telling her that babies had been born for centuries without his help.... *O God...help!*

CHAPTER THREE

She did not call back. It had been a week since he left the message on her uncle's answering machine in Bedford, England. The message had assured him someone would call...no one had. He had tried again and again.

Now as he finished supper with Dave and Sherry, he noted their easy comradery...their obvious devotion to one another...how Dave's dark good looks contrasted with Sherry's blonde curls.

"Why don't I just give Leanne a call? The Witherington wedding will be a big affair... could go on for days...the only son...you know...." his brother-in-law grinned. "I doubt it's intentional; she may not even have gotten the message."

Brett nodded as they rose from the table and headed for the den. "How shall we go about this?" he asked, "Will you talk to her first and see if...?"

Dave nodded as he reached for the cordless.

"Hi, Dave...saw your number so I picked it up. How's everyone there?"

"We seem to be doing okay...we're sure wondering how you are, Leanne."

"Well...I have to admit there's not as much of me as there used to be...and not nearly as much as I'd like...but I think I'm gaining on it."

"Lee...uh...tell me...uh...why you ran away without telling us."

"That's an easy one. You would have tried to stop me."

"You got that right! You might at least have left a note for Brett...."

"I doubt he knows I'm gone. Besides, I wasn't really sure I'd be going to England when I left for Toronto. I needed to recoup and I certainly went to the right place. Billie's a jewel...and this is a healing place, too, with Auntie Beth being a celiac...I'm learning a lot about caring for myself...."

"I'm glad to hear that, Lee. You certainly need to rest and recover from your ordeal. So, you arrived in time for the wedding? Did it go well?"

"The best! Uncle Charles didn't spare the horses, as they say. I had never seen Martyn look so sophisticated...definitely upper crust," she chuckled, "not like him at all. Course I couldn't take in all the festivities...I only lasted through about half."

"Good to hear... good to hear that all went well. So..." he began again, "when can we expect you home?"

"I have no reason to hurry back to Toronto."

"Why Toronto? I'm talking home...as in London, Ontario."

"I have no such plans."

"I hope you're kidding me. Are you planning to talk this over with Brett?"

"Why would I do that? Brett hasn't talked to me in months...he's not interested in me, or any of my plans," her voice became more emphatic as she talked, "besides...it will be weeks before he even realizes I'm not there...."

"That isn't true, Lee," he cut in "He missed you the day you left and started looking. You must know he tried to call you in Bedford and left a number."

"Odd! Why would he do that?" she avoided the question.

"Why don't you ask him?" he suggested as he handed the phone to Brett.

They both heard the click. Stricken, Brett stood clutching the cordless phone.

"Maybe we need to go and get her," Dave suggested as they discussed what he had just heard.

"I've already thought of going after her. What would happen if I just showed up on the doorstep? Would they let me in?"

Dave pondered. "Depends on whether Lee would approve. She

has her uncle and aunt wrapped around her little finger. Aunt Beth never had a daughter and always favoured Leanne. Since Mom and Dad are gone...you get the picture? And she is a lawyer, after all, she'd be outraged!"

Brett nodded slowly. "You got that right. I would certainly need her permission to visit. If she won't even take my call...I guess I know where I stand."

"Maybe you two should just leave her be...give her time to get well," Sherry suggested as she set coffee and butter tarts on the desk. "And she does need time with her aunt...she needs to learn all about celiac disease and how to handle it. Maybe I'll go and see her myself, and take Mandy...." She stopped as the phone interrupted her thoughts.

"Hi, Sherry, this is Lee. What is this...a conference call? Please tell Dave for me that I'm not impressed with his trying to force Brett to talk to me. Brett obviously knows where I am...if he wanted to talk to me...."

"Leanne...please don't hang up on me. I need to talk to you. I've tried a number of times. Please...can I call you from home in a half hour?"

She started as she recognized Brett's tearful plea. "Fine," was all she could manage.

What have I done? I should never have called back, she remonstrated. *What could we possibly have to talk about? Guess I'd best spend the next half hour in prayer...O Lord, God, you know what's going on in Brett's heart...and in my own. Help me to know what to do. I can't believe he wants to talk to me. You know that for four months....* She broke off as sobs shook her slender frame. *I didn't think I had any tears left...any feelings; now I hear Brett sobbing...I didn't think the man had an honest emotion.... O Lord God, please...help me know what You would do.*

The phone rang as she tried desperately to compose herself. "Thank you, God, that Auntie and Uncle are out," she whispered as she picked it up on the third ring..

"This is Leanne."

"Lee, sweetheart...I'm so sorry that I've been out of it for so many months...I...I....need to talk to you. Can I come and see you?"

"See me? Here? In Bedford? Whatever for?"

"I need to talk...we need to talk...."

"About what, Brett? I was available for four months...twenty-four hours a day...and I couldn't buy a minute of your time. Now that I'm half way around the world...."

"I know...I know...and I'm...." he paused, struggling for words to describe his grief.

"You're what, Brett?"

"Well, I'm seeing someone now, and...."

"So you're seeing Rhonda?"

"Rhonda! Whatever would make you think such a thing?"

"Come now, Brett. A little dose of honesty might be refreshing. She was in your office three times when I called...three times when you were too busy to take my call."

"Leanne, that's not true. Where did you get a notion like that?"

"The secretaries—twice from Melva, once from Becky."

"Well, there is some truth to it...but not the way you're thinking...you need to let me explain...we need to get together."

"What is it you want, Brett? What is so important that it can't wait until I get back to Toronto? Do you want a divorce?"

"A divorce? No...That's not an option. Please, Lee, let me come... I can't go on...."

"I have a long way to go before I'm ready to take on the pain of the last five or six months, Brett. Right now I'm operating on numb...it's all I can manage. As I mentioned to Dave, I don't expect to return to London...and since you're already seeing someone else...I really don't see the point."

"No, Lee, no. I'm not seeing a woman...it's not like that...I'm seeing a man—he's...I mean...."

"O God, help...." she said as she put the phone down and burst into tears.

She let it ring until the answering machine cut in. "Leanne...please pick up the phone. The doctor I'm seeing is a Christian psychologist...you know...I saw him before we were married...Dr.

Paul Hayes. He's helping me...trying to help me figure out what happens to me that makes me numb out...please...."

She picked up the phone, "Brett, I'm sorry. I'm really in no condition to discuss this. Leave me alone, please. I'm not able to...to get a handle on things...." she finished tearfully.

"Oh, Kitten, I am so sorry to have put you through this. Will you call me sometime...when you can, I mean?"

"I don't know. I really don't know. I just want to be left alone. Please tell Dave."

"I love you, Lee. I'll do whatever you want. Please...don't shut me out forever."

CHAPTER FOUR

It's been five weeks since I talked to her...she may well be back in Toronto...semester is over ...condo should be empty...tenants gone. Maybe I'll call Bill and Billie and see if they know, he mused as he headed into the city for his weekly appointment with Dr. Hayes.

Paul Hayes had become a good friend in the months since the counselling sessions began...or rather continued. He was blessed to have someone like him to go to. After all, it was Paul who had counselled him before his marriage when the awful dreams had driven him to distraction. Together they had uncovered the horrible abuse he had experienced in the group home...and the dreams had ceased.

All the more puzzling that they were recurring now. Not that they were the same...this seemed to be something even more sinister...more vicious...dreams that threatened to turn him into a wife abuser. He shuddered as he remembered the night he woke to find himself standing beside the bed–looming over Lee with a belt clenched in his fist. Was he sleepwalking? And why would he do such a thing? His fear had driven him to move out of the bedroom...into the guest room. That much he remembered. If only he could get a handle on the dream...on what had been going around in his subconscious! And why he had subsequently numbed out his emotions.

No use if-only-ing myself to death, he decided. He would go over it again with Paul today. The counsellor had suggested it might be profitable to have Leanne come in for a chat–she might be able to shed some light. He had agreed that it was worth a try, then remembered thinking, *Fat chance! She won't even talk to me!*

That was another good session; I'm glad I came. He sat in the BMW in the parkade, contemplating the discussion with Paul. *He gives me reason to hope. And I did promise him I would try to contact Leanne before I leave the City...since Bill says she's back. Perchance she may agree to an interview. Guess I won't know till I try. Best try her cellular first...she probably has an unlisted number at the condo.*

"The customer you have dialed is not standing by," a recording informed him.

"Fine," he muttered. "Maybe I'll just drive by."

A late-model deep-purple Lexus stood on the driveway. *New*, he decided. *It can't belong to Lee...she wouldn't have the money...she hasn't even drawn a salary for months. So...maybe it's time to find out.* He parked behind the purple wonder and waved at the neighbour as he moved toward the front door.

His mind reeling, he eyed the young man in cut offs–his tawny hair sweated and curling around his ears. Obviously he was very much at home...relaxed...sure of himself...confidence oozing from his tanned face and muscular shoulders to his bare feet.

"How can I help you?" he asked with a very British accent

Suddenly finding his voice, Brett managed, "Leanne...I would like to see Leanne."

"I'm sorry...she is not here at the moment. Can I take a message?"

"Do you know when she will be back?"

"You will need to tell me who you are," he began as Leanne arrived from her run. She was in cut offs, too, Brett noticed. Her hair–still that deep auburn–was longer than he remembered and tied back; sweat beaded her forehead and soaked her tee shirt.

"Hello, Brett," she said, waving the barefoot friend inside. "What can I do for you?" she asked, as he stood speechless.

"I....uh...I'm...uh...wondering," he paused, a million questions assaulting him at once. "Would it be possible for us to get together...some things...I'm wondering...would you have time...?"

"I could meet you at McDonald's in a half hour," she suggested, "once I've had time to shower and change."

"I'd be happy to wait," he began hopefully.

"No need, I'll meet you there."

"He sure knows how to pick 'em," he muttered as he passed the Lexus in the driveway.

"Both cars and women." He backed out slowly, "McDonald's," he snorted as he drove away. "Why do I always wind up spilling my guts at McDonald's?"

He watched her park the purple wonder and move toward the restaurant...not missing how lovely she looked in her khakis and tan shirt. Her hair–now loosened–hung in a soft pageboy framing her face. She had not regained all that she lost, but her figure....

He rose as she entered and stood while she seated herself. "Thank you for seeing me," he began. "Can I get you something?"

"Just coffee. I can't eat anything else here," she responded.

He remembered then...nothing with gluten...no flour. "So...would you like to try somewhere else?"

"No, coffee's fine," she cut him off.

He's still as handsome as ever; she surveyed his six-foot physique as he stood at the counter. *No wonder I fell so hard! He's lost weight. Looks a little older...no grey among that gorgeous sandy hair...maybe he's just stressed...thought I was over him by this time....*

Please God, he prayed as he collected the coffees. *We're not getting off to a very good start.*

"Leanne," he began as they stirred their coffee. "You are looking so lovely...I trust that means you're feeling better?"

She nodded. "Coming along. I'm trying to get back in shape...get my strength back. Guess it just takes more time and energy than I expected. So...what did you want to talk about?" she asked, cutting through the small talk and getting right to the point.

"Leanne," he tried to take her hand and she moved back slightly, "I...I guess...I need to know what your plans are...how I can help...if there's anything I can do."

"I plan to continue the master's scholarship, Brett, and no, I don't think there's anything you can do for me."

"What about finances, Lee? I notice that you haven't touched your salary...."

"What do you mean, salary? I haven't worked for six months or more...how could I possibly...?

"You were entitled to six-months salary for maternity leave."

"I didn't know, Brett, and I was way too ill to care; no-one else cared enough to let me know."

O God, help...I'm in over my head again! "Lee, you have to believe that if I could turn back the clock...."

"There's a few things that I would do differently too, Brett."

"I'm afraid to ask what."

"It's just as well. We both have regrets, I'm sure."

Trying a new tack, he continued, "Can I ask what you plan to do when you finish the master's program?"

"I don't know. I guess we'll just have to wait and see."

"Leanne," he sought her eyes...still that beguiling green, he noted, before she looked away. "Do you plan...is it your intention...to...to...." he fumbled, afraid to ask what he desperately needed to know.

"Probably not in this lifetime," she answered. "I'm sorry, Brett. If what we had is marriage...I'm definitely not cut out for it."

"Leanne...Kitten...we were happy...incredibly happy...until...."

"Until I got sick, Brett, and needed a husband's love. Then your promises of 'till death' disappeared along with you."

"It's not the way you think, Lee. I wish I could explain what happened the night...."

"You need to take responsibility for your actions. You're too big a boy to hide behind dreams and use them to excuse your bad behaviour."

She stopped at the look on his face. "I'm trying, Kitten. If you won't let me help you, will you help me?"

"How do you propose I do that?"

"Doctor Hayes thinks you might be able to shed some light on our situation. Would you ...would you be willing to talk to him about us...about me?"

She sat silently for some time, staring into her empty coffee mug. "If you think that will help, Brett...yes...if you think that will help...I'll talk to him."

"Thank you, I appreciate your willingness," he tried a smile as she rose to go. "How can I get in touch?"

"My cell phone...it's usually on."

He resisted reminding her that it hadn't been on today. The time she had allotted him was obviously up, and neither of them had even mentioned the tanned bombshell in cutoffs.

CHAPTER FIVE

Thursday again. He sat contemplating the busy-ness of the past week. Tomorrow he would head into Toronto...another session with Paul Hayes. He wondered if Leanne had been in and how an exchange of information would play out between them. He bowed his head, his elbows on the desk, his head in his hands. *Please, God, don't let us mess up worse than we have already. I believe we belong together...I believe you brought us together. You know I love Lee and I think she still loves me. Guide us, please, God. Give us wisdom...we don't know what to do.*

The intercom interrupted his prayer. "Mrs. Carter is here to see you."

What could she possibly want this time? We finished her husband's estate weeks ago, he mused. "Show her in, please, Becky."

As Beverly Carter asked the same questions and he gave the same answers as last week, he found himself wondering about the purpose of her visits. Each time she seemed to get more personal, enquiring about his health, expressing concern over the long hours he kept, calling him "Brett."

He had begun to straighten up his desk and close the file, indicating that the appointment was over, when she leaned across the desk, and enquired, "Do you work late on Fridays, too, or might you have time to join a lonely lady for supper?"

Her invitation caught him by surprise. He sat for a moment trying to think of a way to excuse himself with the least embarrassment to both parties.

Seeing his hesitation as indecision, she pressed as coyly as she could. "I'm really quite a good cook, you know, and I do know how to make a tired executive relax," she smiled seductively.

"Mrs. Carter," he began.

"Please...it's Bev."

"Mrs. Carter," he began again, "My wife is studying in Toronto and I'm sure she'd take a rather dim view of my accepting an invitation to dine alone with an attractive lady. I usually spend my week-ends in Toronto."

"I'm sorry. I had heard that...that was over. I mean...I thought you were single again...or going to be. I...." Her face turned crimson at the look of astonishment, then anger on his.

"Well, now you know it isn't true. Thank you for your kindness but, as I have explained, it is quite impossible. I am very married...and I have no desire to be otherwise."

As the door closed behind her, he muttered, "Please God, answer my prayer soon."

CHAPTER SIX

He seated the shapely young woman, noting how beautifully the soft tones in her suit complimented her rich auburn hair. *She's some gorgeous! No wonder Brett has his shirt in a knot to get her back!*

"I want to thank you for taking time to come in, Mrs. Walker," he began. "I know a little about the pressures of post-graduate work."

"I'm glad to do what I can," she answered. "Please call me Leanne."

"Certainly, if you'll call me Paul."

She nodded as he continued.

"Would you be uneased if I were to record our conversation?" At her questioning look, he explained, "I like to do this so I can listen to it again if I need to...or you can have a copy if you wish. And with your permission, I would share it with Brett. Would you object to any of those reasons?"

She considered for a few moments. "No, I don't object. I would say the same things if Brett was listening."

"Perhaps you might begin by telling me how you met Brett. I understand you are also a lawyer and have worked together?"

"Yes...and yes. I'm a lawyer...I have worked with Brett and my brother David, his partner. I met Brett when I still had almost a year of studies to complete at U of T. He needed an executive assistant and an old friend of the family, Judge Ben Davis, suggested he give me a call.

"I'm sorry, I need to back up a bit. I had taken a year off from University of Toronto to care for my father. He and Mom had been in a car accident the year before. Mom died instantly, but Dad lived

29

another 15 months or so before he died of his injuries. During that period I cared for him and helped him clear up a lot of loose ends with his practice. We moved his office to our home and worked together as long as he was able." She paused as tears threatened to escape.

"I am indeed saddened...perhaps we could...."

"No, it's fine. I'm fine. I just wanted you to know why I wasn't in school when Brett called. I had taken two courses from University of Western Ontario in London, and had only a couple of classes and exams to finish when I agreed to work for Brett for the summer. I'll never forget the interview. It was quite awful."

She noticed that a small smile playing about his lips as he invited her to continue.

I bet Brett has already told him about this. "I was caught completely by surprise...he was incredibly handsome...gorgeous hair ...deep blue eyes...tanned...and etcetera," she paused as she realized that the man to whom she spoke also shared many of those characteristics. She flushed slightly as she continued, "He showed me in, motioned me to a chair and started questioning me. His manner wasn't especially polite or kind and in fact he became quite sarcastic. I couldn't think of one good reason why I should sit and listen, never mind work for him, so I simply got up and headed for the door. I remember the surprise on his face as he suggested I take a seat since he wasn't done. I also remember telling him that he was 'quite done'."

"And then?"

"Well, he apologized and I went to work for him because he seemed so desperate. His files were piling up and he had just taken on a criminal case. I did think, though, that in view of his need for help...he might at least have tried to be civil."

"I would think so."

"I guess that's a rather lengthy explanation as to how we met. Our relationship continued to be stormy. He was just not a nice man! And he resented me...or maybe he resented that he needed anyone."

"But somewhere along the way, that changed?"

"Slowly. He finally laid a few of his suspicions to rest, concerning my motives, and I agreed to stay the summer if he quit attacking me. It was indeed an interesting time in my life. He never ceased trying to date me."

"Trying?"

"Yeah. He succeeded from time to time, but I was too scared of him...well, maybe I was too scared of my attraction to him...."

"So you were attracted to him?"

"Oh, definitely. I had never been that attracted to a man...and he's a lot of man! But he seemed so angry inside...it was always there just waiting for an excuse to get out. And he was so close-mouthed about his past...I couldn't enjoy his attentions...I felt at odds with myself. I wanted a relationship with him...terribly...but I couldn't give myself to it."

"You certainly express yourself very well, Mrs...Leanne. Tell me why you changed your mind and became Mrs. Walker."

"After a particularly difficult time in our relationship, Brett recommitted his life to Christ. His whole life changed. He had changed a lot before then and we had been dating steadily."

"This difficult time you speak of...is that when another woman...? Brett has shared a little about this. Would you like to share your version?"

"Do you really think this might be helpful?"

He nodded, and she began, "I met Rhonda Fleming at University of Western Ontario when we were both taking night classes. Of course it was when my father was ill and I was caring for him during the day. Rhonda was pregnant and very distressed. She had been used by her father, a lawyer, since she was quite young and was a very hurting woman. She had become morally loose and enjoyed attracting and exploiting men, particularly lawyers."

"I can see that happening."

"She lived with us for a short while...then aborted the little one...and carried on with her lifestyle of men and drugs. My father was unable to cope with her smoking and her behaviours and we had to ask her to leave. She threatened to get even.

"Shortly after I started back to University of Toronto, she began to article with a legal firm down the hall from Brett. By now my brother was articled with Brett and was not a little concerned when he realized Rhonda had hit upon Brett as her next victim."

"Can you describe 'hit upon'?"

"Well...I wasn't there, of course, but from the way Brett described it...and Dave...she would join him at lunch in Tim Horton's, or Wendy's or wherever, pretending to come upon him by coincidence. Then she began coming to the office with small matters that would hardly need a lawyer...she followed up with an invitation to join her for a week-end at her father's cabin at Port Franks."

Noting his smirk, she asked suddenly, "Are you enjoying this?"

"I'd have to say that I am."

"So, you've heard this from Brett. Am I telling the same story?"

"Very much so! How did you respond to all of this?"

"Not very well, I'm afraid."

"Please...go on. Tell me...."

"I guess I didn't mention that I had gone to England for a couple of weeks in August to visit my aunt and uncle...but also to have some time alone...sort out my feelings for Brett...think through my future...where my life might take me if I continued my relationship with him...all that sort of thing. I prayed a great deal about it...worked through a lot of scenarios...."

"Such as?"

"Well...I looked at the gifts God had built into my life, and asked Him how He would want me to use them to serve Him and others. I reviewed my education...my experience...my heritage...the expectations of those who know me...know me well. I believed all of those things had a part in shaping me. But I kept coming back to the fact that I am a woman and that my body was prepared by God to bear children. As women we bear the responsibility to pass on the 'torch of life' if you will...so there will be a next generation...." She looked questioningly at him to see if he comprehended.

"Wow! What an interesting observation! I've never heard it expressed like that before... actually hadn't even thought of it in that way."

"I guess that's a very long explanation...why I felt the Lord approved of my relationship with Brett. It changed my attitude toward him and I couldn't wait to get home. He met me at the airport...and..." her face flushed as she remembered, "and I realized I didn't want to live without this man in my life. I had certainly fallen in love."

"So the Lord gave you the green light?"

"I certainly thought so at the time. He came nearly every week-end...we looked forward to being together...had great times of fun...talking...."

"What changed?"

"Looking back on it, I think it might have been a process. He never seemed interested in the decisions I had made in England...in fact he avoided any intimate talk about our relationship ...yet he nearly wore the tires off that snazzy BMW coming to see me. He certainly acted like a man in love...."

"Did he ever tell you he loved you?"

"No," she shook her head. "No, he didn't. I guess...I felt that while he liked me well enough, he was simply not ready to commit and maybe...never would be. He had been alone for years...avoided any entanglements...." She shrugged her shoulders and looked at Paul.

"Go ahead ."

"I was surprised, though...make that shocked...when he told me he had been invited to spend Thanksgiving week-end at the beach, and that he was planning to go. I thought he was kidding at first. By the time I found out he wasn't kidding and that the woman was Rhonda...."

"Keep going."

"I just fell apart. I couldn't believe he had spent the whole day toying with me as though I was the only woman in the world...and all the while he planned to week-end with Rhonda. I don't remember what I said but he accused me of being jealous...got very angry with me...and I fled."

"Fled?"

"Into the house and locked the door."

"Why did you not stay and talk it through?"

"I'm not sure. I thought his mind was made up. And...and...I don't know...but I guess I've never really had to deal with such deep emotional issues. It was different than dealing with the death of Mom and Dad, and then Brody–he was a little neighbour boy with cerebral palsy; I used to play with him a lot and take care of him when I was still in school. I should just mention in passing that his mom, Melva, now works in the offices of Walker and Stevenson. I hired her to be my secretary after Brody died."

"Can you explain the difference?"

"Maybe," she said after some serious thought. "Maybe...I guess I felt that I had misread the Lord's will...that I wanted so much to have his permission that...that I just took it," she finished in a whisper. "I thought I had gotten to know Brett...and then I didn't know him at all."

He nodded. "So then?"

"He didn't go on the week-end after he discussed it with my brother, Dave. Then he recommitted his life to Christ."

"And you forgave him?"

"I did. And he forgave me for being so impetuous. But I didn't really feel that I should continue...that we should continue the relationship. I was no longer sure that I had read the Lord correctly, and I certainly didn't know Brett like I thought I did."

"How did he respond...I mean, did he accept that...find it satisfactory to...?"

"Not at all. He wanted to renew the relationship. I expect he felt that I was making him pay...hadn't really forgiven him."

"So?"

"Well, I guess you know about the professor that stalked me...and traumatized me?"

"Lonnie Hencken. Yes, I'm familiar. He actually attacked you at one point, didn't he?"

"Yes, but he warned me and threatened me many times and finally decided to just come and get me. I was so frightened I could hardly concentrate on my studies. So I asked the Lord to show me that I was protected...to give me some sign to ease my stress...my fear."

"And did He?"

The tears that had been threatening now spilled over. "He sent Brett."

"Oh my! Oh my! The plot thickens."

"Indeed, it did. I could hardly believe that God had sent Brett to answer my prayer. And He answered one I hadn't prayed yet, 'What shall I do about Brett?' I felt He had just given me permission to let Brett back into my life."

"And then a few months later?"

"Yes. He proposed at Christmas time and we planned to marry in June." She looked at her watch. "I'm sorry I have to run...I'm not sure that preamble...."

"Thank you. You have shed a lot of light. Can you come again next week? Same time?"

"That should be okay."

"Would you like to take the tape of Brett's session?"

"No thank you," she replied as she moved gracefully toward the door.

CHAPTER SEVEN

He could hardly wait to see Paul today. Leanne had given permission for him to listen to her recorded session with the psychologist. *I feel like a high schooler on his first date,* he decided.

After a few words of greeting, Paul suggested they go over it together and turned on the tape.

He closed his eyes as he listened to her voice...professional...yet not sacrificing the warm, vibrant feeling that was so much her. He could see her sitting there as she spoke, leaning ahead from time to time to make a point...wiping a tear now and then when her voice broke.

He smirked and nodded at Paul as she described their meeting and his manner of interviewing her.

Paul stopped the tape. "Help me to understand. Why so angry and insolent with such a lovely little lady?"

"I've thought about that plenty. I think it was because I was so attracted to her...that hadn't happened to me before...I was numb, as you know...self sufficient. She's probably right when she suggests that I was angry because I needed someone to help in the office. She thought it was because I resented her salary. Not so. It was that she got under my skin...made me feel something for her...it infuriated me."

"But you tried to date her?"

"Yeah. I tried to date her. Wouldn't you?"

"You bet! But help me to understand this love-hate relationship."

"Don't think I can. I didn't understand it myself. I pulled her to me and pushed her away at the same time. She was delightful to have in the office and I dreaded the day she would leave. The clients loved her. I found myself angry and indignant when guys tried to flirt with her. She was obviously experienced...knew how to say 'no' without causing offence. One of my clients, a Chinese import-export millionaire never quit trying for a date. He had it all and he knew how to use it; he was handsome, well-built, well-dressed. Did I mention charming? I was afraid to get out of ear shot, for fear he'd succeed."

"So you were fond of her from the start?"

"That's a mild term," he smirked.

"Do you know how this transformation came about...when the pull began to take over the push?"

"Well, I think the fact that she walked out on me during the interview...and again when she visited me in the hospital and I took a slice out of her. She stated matter-of-factly that I was cruel, and she left. The night I was discharged, I stopped at the office around 8:00 and she was working. Surprised, I asked what she was doing there at that hour. She took offense and was gone in seconds. I wasn't used to having women walk out on me...I usually had the opposite problem...but she played by a different script." he paused, fishing for just the right words. "Somewhere between the last two 'leavings' I began to realize that I didn't want her leaving–ever!"

"So?"

"So, I collected my car from the parking garage, picked up a pizza and went to her house. She invited me in out of the rain, accepted my pizza, and offered coffee and soup. Her brother, Dave, arrived home from U of T shortly after. I discovered that I had instructed a couple of his classes when he was a freshman, and we hit it off. Before the visit ended, he agreed to consider taking his articles with me."

"You're quite a man, Walker...not bad for an hour's work! What happened with Leanne?"

"We called a truce–she'd give me one more chance if I'd lay down the hatchet."

Paul grinned. "That's incredible!" He touched the switch and she continued her story.

He noticed Brett's unease and heightened colour as she described his behaviour when she returned from England...then his decision to week-end with Rhonda.

"I know we've already talked about this," Paul remarked, "but do you have anything further to say now that you've heard Leanne?"

"Not a whole lot, I guess. As I told Leanne, later, I had been in love with her for a long time. I don't really know why I didn't say so...maybe I was afraid of her rejection...or as she suggests...maybe I was afraid of commitment. That doesn't seem right though; I wanted to be part of a family so badly...I wanted a family of my own. I really thought that I didn't say so because I wanted it to be a special occasion...a celebration of our love for each other. Now I wonder if I procrastinated because I wasn't sure that she shared my feelings. You know, we never did discuss the decisions she made in England...nor the incredible process...prayer and all...that she went through just to date me. I remember her saying that she was very careful about making decisions, but she didn't sweat the small stuff." He grinned. "Guess that must mean she didn't see me as small stuff."

"Indeed, she did not! She's quite something!"

"That she is!"

"So, in view of your obvious love for Leanne, I'm having difficulty understanding the Rhonda thing."

"Come on now. We've already talked about that. I agreed to go because it sounded like quite a few legal people would be there. Originally it sounded like she was inviting both of us...then she apologized...she had run out of room for another single woman. I should have clued in, but when she said she knew Leanne, I thought it would be okay to go. I even thought that Leanne would be pleased that I would help out her friend. Apparently her boy friend had stood her up. The rest is history. Leanne was upset when I told her about it...then she nearly went into shock when she found out it was Rhonda. I got angry...she shut the door in my face."

"Describe your feelings?"

"Shut out...misunderstood...exasperated. She wouldn't answer the phone...I tried to call her on the cell while I sat on the driveway. Women! Finally I left."

"Feelings as you drove away?"

"Anger at her...anger at myself for having acted like a jerk. I asked myself what I would feel like if she did that to me. Overwhelming sadness...a great emptiness as I drove back on the 401."

"So, as a result of this, you committed your life to Christ?"

"That's a brief little phrase...neat little parcel of words to describe my pain...soul searching...despair. Dave worked me over and he didn't let me away with much. I had asked Christ into my life when I was a kid at camp, but I really had no one to disciple me, and I didn't know the Scriptures, so it was high time I did. Dave made me understand that I couldn't bargain with God...go through the motions to get Leanne back. He suggested that I put her in God's hands...and leave our relationship with Him."

"So...did you?"

"I tried. I was very sincere. I really tried . I asked her forgiveness. She said she forgave me, but she didn't feel she should continue with our relationship. Then I heard about Hencken and that he intended to have her one way or the other. The guy was a predator from way back; he should have been behind bars years ago, but nobody reported him. His students were afraid he'd fail them. The Dean didn't have enough hard evidence–or maybe not enough backbone–to use what he had. Dave and I agreed that I needed to be on hand to protect her."

"What were you thinking as she described this scenario?"

"My coming to protect her? Well, I just came. She would never have granted permission. She is independent and then some. She refuses to allow her brother to 'bully' her, as she puts it. Actually Dave isn't a bully, but he may have been overly protective when she was small. She will have none of it! But, what strikes me quite forcefully in her story is the way she consulted the Lord about everything and let Him direct her. I had no idea...you know what I mean...that she agonized over her decisions to date me...to allow me back into her life. She certainly kept me at arms length while she and God talked it over," he laughed.

"Good for her! Do you think she's asking God about you now?"

"I hope she is. Her refusing to listen to my story is...unsettling, to say the least. When I met with her...in McDonald's...."

"McDonald's?"

"Yeah. She always wants to meet at McD's...and she can't even eat the food...most of it has gluten...and she's a celiac...allergic to wheat and stuff."

"Why do you think she chooses McDonald's?"

"She worked there when she was a kid...just for work experience, I think. I don't know why she still goes there...maybe she's comfortable...." he shrugged his shoulders.

"Sorry, I got you off track there. You were saying?"

"She told me that she didn't think..." he hesitated as he tried to control the tremor in his voice, "... she didn't expect us to be back together in this lifetime."

"Has she ever said things like that before?"

Brett shook his head. "Never."

"You mentioned how she prays, or has in time past, about her relationship with you. Do you? Do you pray about this, Brett? Do you ask God if...?"

"No. Not 'if'. I don't ask Him 'if'. Leanne is my wife...it's already the Lord's plan that we be together. I just ask Him 'how?'"

Paul nodded. "Let's bring this to Him again before you go."

CHAPTER EIGHT

He drove slowly, savouring the sound of his wife's voice on the tape. He grinned as she told of her attraction to him and described him as "a lot of man." He rewound it...and ran it over again. He wished he could have watched her when she said that. Was she smiling? She sounded so warm...like he knew her to be...not like the persona she had donned for her meeting with him.

The meeting turned his thoughts to the purple Lexus...the playboy in cutoffs. He hated him already. "Wretch," he muttered, "how dare he move in with my wife! And Lee...doesn't seem like her to bring back a Brit for a boyfriend. She makes decisions so slowly...carefully". It occurred to him she may have met him before they were married...the summer she went to visit her aunt and uncle. *Did she get to know him then? Date him? And that blasted car! How did he know she was fanatic about purple? He must have known her for a while...knew she needed a car. Why didn't I get her a car? Why didn't she ask for one if she wanted one?* He felt his tension increase with the agitated thoughts...his gut tied in knots. *Guess I'd better watch my driving,* he concluded as a car pulled in front and he touched the brakes.

He listened again to her account of his planned weekend with Rhonda. Then made the connection to her accusation when he called her in England...that he was seeing Rhonda on a regular basis...she had called the office three times and he was too busy to see her...because Rhonda was in his office. *If only she'd let me tell her about it...or listen to my tape. She knows how to put a guy on ice. Guess I should have thought about that before I did that to her. I*

41

wonder if Dave could do something. He remembered that she had asked Dave not to call her when she was in England. Did that still apply? He'd just have to find out.

"Lee, it's Dave. I'm on my way to Toronto and I'd like to take you to supper. I should be there around 5:30. Will you call my cell when you get in?"

She clicked off the answering machine and heaved a deep sigh. *Leave it to big brother... guess I knew he'd come sooner or later.* She debated her next move. *Guess I can't run forever...I'll just let him say his piece and get it over with.*

She couldn't help notice the tension in his voice. *He was afraid I wouldn't call,* she thought as they exchanged greetings. He was on the outskirts of Toronto; may take him an hour or so depending on traffic.

She smiled as he suggested they not eat at McDonald's. "Only because they don't have anything I can eat," she joked.

"Lee, I'm really sorry that we haven't...that I haven't...been in touch," he finished as the waitress left with their order. Birkley's Steak House was definitely upstream and she appreciated Dave's choice...though his motive might well be suspect...a secluded spot where they could talk undisturbed. She waited for him to continue...neither rescuing nor encouraging him with the awkward situation he was about.

"I know we've both been busy," he continued, "and...and...I wasn't sure that you wanted to see me after...after...my phone call to England." He stopped...looked at her...and waited for a reply that he was sure would come. It didn't.

"Help me out here," he continued.

"What would you like from me, Dave?"

"I...uh...I...guess I'd like to have my sister back for starters. Lee...I...uh...I guess I'm afraid to talk to you for fear...."

He hesitated so long she prompted, "for fear?"

"That you get up and leave."

"Fear not, big brother. Say on."

"Are you sure about that?"

"Go for it."

"Can I ask you to explain some things I don't understand?"

"Of course," she nodded.

"Can you tell me why you ran away from all of us...why you left Brett?"

"I didn't leave Brett, David. I left an empty house where I had been a prisoner...a very sick prisoner...for more than four months. I wasn't kidding when I said that it would be months before he missed me. If he ever came home, it was after I was asleep...left before I woke. If I called the office he was too busy to talk to me...three times he had Rhonda in his office and couldn't be disturbed. How would he ever know whether I was home or not?"

"He did know, Lee. He rushed home from the office after he heard you asking for help on the answering machine the night the baby...came," he finished lamely. "They were just putting you in the ambulance and he followed to the hospital. He called me on his cell and I met him there...." he looked up at her, his eyes full of tears.

Stop that! Stop those wretched tears. I have no intention of letting you get to me.

"Sherry called her folks and Uncle Ben and Aunt Maude. They all came to the hospital. Bob came from his friend's wedding...complete with camera. We waited...and prayed most of the night while they tried to stabilize you...enough so they could take the baby. They didn't have a lot of hope for either of you." Tears now ran freely down his cheeks and he swiped at them with the huge linen napkin.

"I'm sorry to have put you all through that," she said in an effort to stave off her emotions.

"Lee," he leaned across the table, his voice intense, "what would have happened if Brett hadn't heard the answering machine? You could have died and we wouldn't even know."

Her smirk was cynical. "I could have died at home and you wouldn't have known. Brett simply didn't care. From the time I got sick, he simply ignored me. Why is he making all the fuss now? Because I'm well? Pretending he wants a reconciliation is preposterous!"

"That's not the way it is, Lee."

"Dave, did you come to persuade me to go back to Brett? I know you're his friend...his partner...that's the reason I let him get away with the emotional abuse...why I left without telling anyone. I didn't want to get between you. I know the respect and comradery you share. I couldn't ask Sherry for help...he would have seen her as an accomplice. So, you see, to ask me to return to Brett is foolish. Obviously he's had a girl friend all along."

"That's not true. Brett has not had a girl friend. He has been working at night on his...."

"Rhonda."

"Definitely not. Brett said he tried to tell you about her but you wouldn't listen. Didn't you learn anything from the last time he tried to tell you about her? You ran away from him that time, too, and shut the door in his face, as I recall. If you had listened you would have saved all of us a lot of pain."

She raised her eyebrows as he continued.

"You surprise me, you know. You are a lawyer...a very skilled lawyer, I might add. You're a bearcat for truth...you want justice...you get after Brett and me when you aren't convinced we have all the facts in a case...."

She nodded, "So...where are you going with this? What does that have to do...?" her voice trailed off as she suddenly realized where he was heading.

"You know where I'm going, Lee. You are judging Brett, and I suspect—me as well—and you have only half the story...half the facts...garbled facts to boot."

"Ouch! Ouch!" she echoed, shrinking back as if to avoid a blow. "You sure know how to hammer a gal. I should have known that with two lawyers and a psychologist...."

"Not so, Lee. We love you and you know it. We want you back."

"So...how do you see that happening?"

"You need to get all of the facts first off. Start with the Rhonda thing. You know what she's like. She kept dropping in at the office...this was after the second restraining order expired. We got another and she ignored it. The girls in the outer office couldn't stop her from charging in to see Brett. She wanted him to help her launch a law suit against her father for sexual abuse. He knew she had a case and needed help, and he recommended someone who handles that sort of thing. She was furious; she wanted Brett and refused to take 'no' for an answer. She continually flounced into his office without permission or notice. The one time, Uncle Ben was there. Her behaviour was so bizarre, he suggested psychiatric treatment."

"So?"

"So what?"

"So what happened?"

"So he called the police once and had her removed. It didn't stop her, and he finally had to call 9-1-1. By that time, they simply took her to the hospital. Her dad signed an order that she needed psychiatric help."

"Big of him!"

"You got that right. Got himself out of a peck of trouble...at least for the time being."

"So where is she now?"

"Still in the psychiatric hospital, I believe."

She sat silently trying to digest the information she had just received. "So why didn't anyone ever tell me about this when I called?"

"I'm sorry I can't answer that. I really don't know...except to say that she caused such an upheaval in our normal routine. I'm sorry...I'll have to ask the girls. Guess I thought you knew...strange that I should have thought that. Guess I can understand why Brett wouldn't say anything...knowing how you felt about her...." he paused.

"I really have a great deal of pity for her...have had since she stayed with us...but...as you well know...she is out to destroy men...their wives...me...anybody. I don't know anything about psychiatry...or counselling...or whatever...but without God's intervention, I doubt she can be helped."

"I suspect you're right. But she couldn't be allowed to continue. Better she be where she might get help...and not hurt anybody else. Agreed?"

She nodded.

"I think, Lee, that was the situation the times you called...in fact, I know it was. She came many times. There was nothing going on between her and Brett...no tete-a-tete. Does that help?"

"Dave...did Brett ask you to do this? Are you getting a raise?" she raised an eyebrow.

"Yes, he asked me to intercede for him. No, I'm not getting paid to do it. I was glad to try and talk to you. I love you both so much. Your pain is tearing me apart."

She flinched as his voice broke. "I know, big bro, and I'm so sorry you and Sherry are caught in the middle. I miss you all so much, and my sweet wee niece. How is she?"

"Gorgeous, like her mom."

"Of course."

"Is she walking?"

"O yeah! Runs all over the place...especially to Daddy when he get home." He stopped as tears slid down her face. "Lee, I'm sorry...so sorry. Your beautiful little one...she looked just like you. We all wished you could have seen her...but they couldn't tell how long it might be before you...."

"I know, Dave, I know," she slid her hand onto his large one. "But I did see her...in my dreams. I saw her, Dave. She was wearing a little pink nightie, and a pink blanket with tiny white lambs all over it. She had loads of dark hair. I knew she was gone before I regained consciousness. The angels came for her...." she paused to wipe her tears. "I saw her lift her tiny arms to the angel who hovered near her. She wrapped her gently in her fluffy robe and...and..." she paused again and wept uncontrollably. "I'm sorry...this is hardly supper conversation."

"Tell me, Lee..."

"I'm not sure I can." She looked up through her tears. "She smiled at me, Dave, and waved as they rose...and they were gone."

"That's unbelievable, Lee. I went with Brett to buy the pink blanket and nightie. We couldn't find any at your place. Sherry offered some things, but he wanted to buy something himself. He was so broken...we all were...we had quite the time in the store. And you saw them in your dream?" he asked with a note of incredulity.

She nodded. "I think we should go, Dave. Maybe we can finish the rest of this at home," she indicated her uneaten steak. "I assume you'll spend the night?"

"If that's okay with you. Brett...uh...indicated that you had someone staying with you."

"No matter...there's room for you."

He parked in the double garage beside the purple Lexus. He didn't ask about the black Jetta on the driveway and she offered no explanation.

"No one home...I wonder if there's classes tonight," she offered as he deposited his bag in the guest room she indicated.

"Hi, Sweetheart," he caught his cell phone on the first ring. "Yup. Had a good trip...I'm at Lee's. We just got in from supper. How are my two special girls?"

She tidied up newspapers and textbooks while he continued talking, but he noticed the man-size sandals, sweats, jacket, Sauconys... definitely not hers! *Why doesn't she say something? She's not exactly stressed about my being here.*

"So," she began as she joined him by the fireplace. "What...how...do you see the future in this? What are you expecting of me?"

"Brett tells me that you don't want to believe that a dream was the cause of his numbing out. I think you need to look at that, Lee. Dr. Hayes thinks he saw something from his childhood that was so horrendous he couldn't cope with it, and his mind wiped it out. He went numb. Don't ask me to explain that–ask Dr. Hayes."

"It seems to me, Dave, that you want me to jump back into a relationship that has ruined my life...never mind that he can re-do the damage any time he chooses to have another dream!" She stopped at the look of surprise on her brother's face.

"I don't think it works like that, Sis. When they got to the bottom of the last dream and exposed the reason for it...the dreams ceased. You have to admit he was a new man. I think that will happen again."

"Unless, of course, he has another dream!"

"You can handle that, Lee. I haven't known you to run from anything."

"I don't think I ever ran...until Brett came into my life. I should have kept on running."

"Stop it, Lee. Promise me you will pursue this thing until it gets figured out?"

He stopped as the door flew open, letting in a fresh gust of wind. The young man responsible for it, hurried to close it behind him, then turned with a warm grin. "Hi, there. Sorry to disturb...has Liz arrived?" Definitely a Brit, Dave decided.

"No, sorry. Didn't know where you might be...without your car. Liz wasn't here when we got in."

"I think she's off to a baby thing...shower, or whatever they call it. Somebody picked her up around 7:30. I caught a ride to the gym with Johnny and Maria ."

"Oh, sorry," Lee cut in as Dave rose and extended his hand. "This is my brother, David Stevenson. Dave, this is Ian Blair. Ian's a friend of cousin Martyn. He's studying here...master's program in Phys-Ed something or other," she smirked, looking at Ian to defend himself.

"She knows I'm really in engineering; she makes jollies of me because I wear cut-offs and enjoy running and sports. What a guy has to put up with just to get an education! And I hear you're another of those legal types!" he laughed as Dave nodded.

"That I am...that I am."

"Good to meet you...very good indeed!"

"I need to hit the feathers, Dave. It's been a long and stressful day," she remarked as Ian headed to the shower.

"Guess we won't have a lot of time in the morning, Lee. Can you answer my question before we...?"

"Which one was that?"

"Will you pursue this thing...not close yourself off from all of us?"

"I can't promise a whole lot, Dave, but you're right...I need to look at all the evidence. I can't promise beyond that."

"Tell me something, Lee. Are you struggling...resisting...." he paused, wondering how his question might be perceived, "...because you're looking for a new relationship with someone else?" he finished.

"Not in this lifetime," she replied with cynical surprise.

He gave her a long affectionate hug before she headed up to bed.

CHAPTER NINE

"Lee, it's Brett. Hencken's appeal will be coming up in a few months. He's out of the psychiatric hospital and seeking bail. Can you give me a call when you get in? ...better call my cellular. Thanks a bunch."

So Lonnie Hencken will be before the courts after spending two years in the psych ward! Guess I should have been paying closer attention to the media reports...they wouldn't dare let him out! Would they? They would if the senior Hencken and Mears have their way. Too bad they didn't grant our bid to declare him a dangerous offender...which he is.... She shuddered, remembering his stalking her...his vicious attack that almost cost her life. *And here I am–back in University of Toronto! Yes, I'll call Brett. Lonnie must never be allowed to roam free...ever again!*

His voice was warm and very Brett. She smiled as he enquired how her classes were going, and thanked her for meeting with Dr. Hayes on his behalf. "Lee, Dave and I are working a little late tonight trying to get this thing off the ground. Today was just too wild to get any thinking done. Would you have time to discuss this with both of us if I called you back on the office phone?"

An hour later they had laid the groundwork and Lee was too exhausted to work on her class project. They were not at all sure that Lonnie would be in custody until his trial...his father and law partner were applying for bail. Dave urged her repeatedly to come back to London if bail was granted, though, of course, he and Brett would be opposing it. It occurred to her that Dave might be crying 'wolf' with Brett's approval. *They would love for me to come 'home'–*

whatever that means for me now. Dave knows jolly well what a stir it would cause if I returned to London...but not to Brett. He's a rascal that brother of mine! Still...my options will be rather limited if Lonnie gets bail. I'll certainly want to speak to the bail hearing...along with a few dozen others, I'm sure.

She spent a long time thinking about Brett before she reached for her Bible. Was he really as faithful as Dave made him out to be? And what about this dream? But Dave wouldn't lie...or mislead her...he never had...not in his nature to do that. She would need to come to terms with her feelings for Brett before they collaborated on this court case. They would be spending a great deal of time in each other's company. The thought both thrilled and terrified her. *I'm afraid I might still love him,* she thought miserably. *Well, tomorrow I'll be seeing Dr. Hayes; maybe I'll just ask him about some of this stuff. We need to talk about the dream...and....* She opened her Bible. "Okay, God, let's see what you have to say about all this." She stopped suddenly, realizing it had been a long time since she had asked His opinion on anything.

She noticed her bookmark in the first chapter of James and turned to it expectantly. It had been a while since she placed it there.

"If any one lacks wisdom let him ask of God, who gives freely...."

"Oh, God," she whispered, "I've been so stubborn...so defensive...so afraid...protective of my emotions. Help me to get out of this self-protective mode and put my life back in Your hands. Give me wisdom tomorrow...help me know what to do about Brett."

A peace she had not known in months flooded her spirit as she slipped into a deep and untroubled sleep.

His time with Paul had gone well. He reviewed the memories they had uncovered as he took the ramp onto Highway 401.

"He's a sharp cookie, that Paul," he said half aloud. "I think I've made him earn his money." He smirked. "Strange how the mind works...I would never have made the connection between Lee's pregnancy and Mom's...that I felt numb and fearful when Lee got sick...because Mom was always so white and shaky...and she always lost the babies...and then her life. I think we're beginning to make progress. Thank you, Lord! Forgive me for thinking it might never happen."

He turned on the cassette player.

"That's okay with me, Paul, as long as we get to the dream." Her voice was music to his ears, but he winced as he heard her repeatedly refer to the doctor as "Paul." *I know he likes to be really informal, but he's far too attractive to be so informal with my wife–and being a widower....* He smiled as they continued the discussion.

"Refresh my memory," the voice of the doctor, "how long were you married before you decided to have a family?"

"Fourteen months before I got pregnant."

"And were they happy months?"

"The happiest of my life until that point."

"Were you both happy? Brett...?"

"If he wasn't, I was certainly too naive to notice. His behaviour led me to believe he was very happy in our relationship."

"Such as?"

"Well..." she pondered a few moments, "well, he always spent a lot of time with me...wanted us to do things together. We went to church together...Bible studies...prayed together most mornings and at bedtime. We ate lunch together at work...he often slipped in to have coffee with me between clients. He liked cooking and helping me in the kitchen. Both of us enjoyed exercising, dancing, skiing, travelling, the arts–symphony, drama. We did a lot of socializing with Dave and Sherry, and other couples. I think we were very compatible. If he was unhappy, as I mentioned, I sure didn't know it."

"Can you put a time on when you felt your relationship changed?"

"Oh, sure. When I got pregnant. I was sick from the beginning and he was not happy with me."

"Do I understand from Brett that you didn't want the pregnancy?"

"He may have said that but it's not exactly the way it was. I felt there was something wrong with me and I wanted to get it straightened out before I had a family. He wanted me pregnant...I'm not sure why? At the time, I thought he really wanted a child. When Dave and Sherry were expecting, Sherry just blossomed. You'd have to understand that Sherry is a gorgeous blonde, blue eyed, clear complexion...beautiful at her worst. When she was with child, she was radiant. I think Dave brought her to the office just to show her off. Of course, her little girl is a tiny Sherry, and Brett could hardly leave her alone. I really thought he wanted a child."

"But what do you think now?"

"Now I'm not sure that was the case. The obstetrician flirted with him, and he readily believed that I was just a reluctant mom. I gave in. I've wondered if it's just a man thing–proof of his manhood, or whatever. I did wonder if it gave him a sense of control...or security...that now I would be dependent on him. He had no reason to worry. I had no intentions of anything else. However, in light of his behaviour...." she stopped.

"Behaviour?"

"Well...he was so disappointed in me...far from being able to show me off...he was rather embarrassed that I looked so...bad."

"Describe 'bad'."

"Colourless...just a sickly, drawn look about my face."

"I'm having a hard time imagining you like that."

"I threw up a lot in the first three months...it didn't help!"

"And then?"

"Then he began to withdraw from me."

"Describe 'withdraw'."

"Hm...let's see. Well, he always slept really close to me...sometimes I couldn't get comfortable and I'd try to move away. I'd wake up with his arms holding me so close I could hardly breathe. Then he changed. Seldom cuddled...slept with his back toward me."

"Did he change in other ways?"

"Oh, sure. On the days when I felt well enough to work at the office, he'd pretend I wasn't there. It was embarrassing. The staff noticed it right away...he had been so attentive before. We had always eaten lunch together...either in the office...or out, and I waited for him to go to lunch one day...only to find he'd gone with a client. The girls felt sorry for me."

"Go on."

"I was sure I'd be over the sick part after three months, but I continued to get worse. Brett withdrew completely. I worked on my computer at home and kept in touch with my secretary until I became too ill. I talked to Dave and asked him to take over my incomplete files and share them with Brett. Dave wasn't into wills and estates and I knew it would be hard for him. I'm sure Brett got the brunt of the workload. I don't suppose it helped his disposition any."

"Was this before the dream?"

"I'm not sure when the dream thing happened. I suspect it was the night he moved out of our bedroom. I awoke sometime after midnight–I'm not sure why; maybe I heard something or felt something unusual. I touched the lamp and it came on . He was standing by my side of the bed with his fists clenched and a horrible look on his face. I must have said something or asked him something, because I remember him telling me to get to sleep, and he touched the lamp and turned it off. A few seconds later I heard the guest room door close rather firmly. In the morning he was gone."

"Gone?"

"I assume he went to work, but he left awfully early."

"Did he come home again?"

"At first he came home in the early evening. I made supper a few times but he didn't come...he was always too busy to take my calls at work so I didn't know if I should expect him. When he was still home at 7:00 one morning, I made breakfast. He was ugly. He left without eating. I decided not to make that mistake again...and I guess he did, too; he never left that late again."

"When did you find out you had celiac disease?"

"About the seventh month of the pregnancy they finally found out why my blood was so low–I had so many transfusions I lost track."

"Tell me about celiac. I gather it had a rather negative effect on the baby?"

"Celiac disease is an allergy to gluten...found in wheat, and other grains. The gluten destroys the small hairs in the duodenum–small intestine. That's the main digestive organ. Since the food can't digest properly, the body suffers from malnutrition. That means a lack of calcium, lack of oxygen due to lack of iron, and on and on. All of this affects the fetus and very often causes miscarriage."

"Was your own life in danger at any time?"

"I guess it was a daily thing."

"I understand they wanted you to abort?"

"I couldn't. I could feel her moving and kicking inside me...struggling for her little life ...how could I ever end it without giving her a chance!"

"Were you aware that you could very well have lost your life...given it up for hers?

"I was aware...both of us were in God's hands."

"What did Brett think of having an abortion?"

"I have no idea.."

"You didn't try to discuss it...or consult him?"

Brett could hear her sobs, and he swung the BMW into the McDonald's restaurant complex beside the freeway, and sat with his face in his hands.

"He didn't care what happened to us one way or the other. I tried to get him to discuss the baby with me. The doctors wanted me to give birth in Toronto so the baby could be checked out at Sick Kids Hospital. I got hold of him one day and asked whether he wanted to be present at the birth. Silly question!"

"So? What did he say?"

Brett cringed as he anticipated her reply. He was guilty as charged. "Oh, God, what happened to make me like that?" he sobbed.

"Something about babies being born for centuries without his help."

"Ouch! Was this before you found you were celiac?"

"Yes. Doctors were concerned I wouldn't carry to term."

"So...how did you respond to his indifference?"

"I knew I was on my own. I took steps to protect myself and the baby. While I was still in hospital, I called friends in Toronto and asked if we could come there until I was able to get back into my condo. It was rented to students until the end of April. Doctors felt the baby might have some brain damage from lack of oxygen and wanted her to have every opportunity available. My friend, Billie, is a pediatric nurse and she offered to care for her if I went back to school. U of T graciously granted me the opportunity to work on my master's degree. I had earned a scholarship."

"So, at that point you decided to leave Brett?"

"Not really. I just decided to leave London. Brett had left me months before."

"But he wants you back, doesn't he? Terribly, in fact. Why do you think that is?"

"I'm not sure he does."

"He does, Leanne. Believe me."

"Well...Brett hates to lose. He's an incredible litigator...formidable even. His determination makes him the lawyer he is. When he makes up his mind, he goes after what he wants."

"So he's made up his mind about you?"

"I'm not sure that's the case. If he's interested in reconciliation, it's probably because he's feeling pressure from Dave. Dave is terribly distraught over our separation and he's been pressuring me to come back to London...back to Brett."

"Can you verbalize your feelings about all this?"

"I don't know...I'm not sure I can. I don't understand Brett if he's sincere in having me back. What does he think I have that he might want? In the last year I've lost my health, my husband, my baby, my career, my income, my self-esteem...and my faith is hanging by a thread. What does he want from me?"

"Your heart, Lee."

She pondered his answer as he continued, "Do you see Brett being responsible for all of those losses?"

"He wasn't responsible for my health."

"Do you see him as responsible for the death of your child ...since he didn't want to wait until you were well?"

"Not really. I bear equal responsibility for that...I wanted to please him...I should have realized that he could hardly know what I was feeling...and when the obstetrician couldn't find anything wrong...I can understand...."

"So you see him being responsible for the other losses?"

"I guess I do. My marriage...career...income...even my self-esteem...were all tied up with him. Do I want to put myself in that position again?"

"So you're back at University. What will you do when you graduate? Do I take it that working with Brett and Dave is not on your agenda?"

"Not so far, Paul. I'm not sure what I'll do. I may work on a doctorate. and teach. I'm a teaching assistant now, and I'm enjoying it."

"Brett mentioned that Lonnie Hencken is up for a bail hearing. What will you do if bail is granted?"

"First off, we intend to oppose it. We would like to see him designated 'a dangerous offender'...that way he'll never be free to offend again. I'll be speaking to the hearing, along with a few dozen others, I'm sure."

"And if bail is granted?"

"I'm not sure what I'll do. I'll certainly need to hire a body guard," she laughed uneasily.

"Will you want Brett?"

"I doubt he would be interested."

"You keep saying that, Leanne. Why?"

"I thought I already explained that."

"Indulge me."

"Brett isn't interested in me. He can have any woman he wants. He hasn't lost any of his boyish charm and he turns it on and off at will."

"Why are you so sure he doesn't want you?"

"I did tell you that he goes after what he wants. When he was courting me he came to Toronto so often...as I mentioned...he wore the tires off his BMW. I thought he was in love with me...then...well, when he did the Rhonda thing, I realized I was just a challenge...once he had accomplished what he set out to do, he simply turned his attention elsewhere."

"But he married you?"

"Yeah. Maybe I presented another challenge."

"And you married him?"

"I was in love, though I always felt there was a whole side of him I didn't know anything about. Turned out I was right."

"But if he did pursue you again, Lee?"

"If he pursued me again it would be because of Dave. I've even been wondering if he did it the first time to hang onto Dave. He knew there were other firms making offers and that Dave was a sought-after commodity in the legal world."

"Do you really believe that?"

"I said that I've been wondering–in view of the past year–I've been wondering."

A dull click announced the end of the tape.

Brett sat in the parking lot...immobilized. "Oh God," he breathed, "I didn't know the half...how could I have been so blind? Give me wisdom to know what to do. Guess I need to get home...better pick up a coffee...a bottle of water. I seem to be dehydrated." He noticed his hand shaking as he handed the change to the girl at the drive through.

CHAPTER TEN

Friday at last. He had made it through another week...well almost. In an hour or so he would head to Toronto and another meeting with Paul. His thoughts centred on the discussion between Lee and Paul. Could she really have thought he pursued her because he wanted Dave to work with him? She was at least as sought after in the legal world as her brother. And, another thing–course she didn't know about that–Dave had at one time forbidden him to court his sister.

"Mr. James Wall to see you. He doesn't have an appointment...says it's personal," Becky informed him on the intercom.

"Show him in...I have a few minutes before I go."

The young man reminded him of himself...probably around six feet...well built...sandy hair...blue eyes. He was obviously nervous as he extended his hand, "I'm James Wall, I'm sorry to barge in like this...I've been wanting to come for some time, but...I...I...always seem to chicken out at the last moment."

"Is there something I can do for you?" Brett responded, hoping to put the young man at ease.

"Well...I...uh...I don't really need anything...I just wanted to meet you...I don't know how to say this but...I'm your brother."

"I beg your pardon?"

"I'm your brother. Our mom died when I was born and Dr. Wall and his wife–Rob and Marg–adopted me," he stopped, noting the shock on the lawyer's face.

"I'm sorry, I shouldn't have come...at least not like this. I picked up the phone a dozen or so times...I wanted so badly to meet you...I see you in the papers from time to time...you're quite a lawyer... I...I

..." he fumbled for words, realizing he had gone about it all wrong.

"What makes you think you're my brother?"

"We have the same mom and dad. Dad, that is Dr. Wall, delivered me. Apparently my birth mom knew she was dying...and she knew that dad...my father...had Lou Gehrig's disease, so she asked the doctor to adopt me. Rob and Marg couldn't have kids of their own, so...they took me. I was 22 in March."

"How long have you known this?"

"Just a couple of months. I had commented several times that I looked just like you...when I saw you in the news. Finally Dad told me you were my brother...and he told me the story. Course I always knew I was adopted because my mom died at birth, but I had never been really curious. Said he didn't think you knew about me."

"It never entered my head that I had a sibling. I was ten when Mom died. I knew she was going to have a baby but no one said anything about it after she died. Guess I assumed the child had died with her. I'm sorry to be so numb but...it will take a while to soak in." He couldn't mention that one more shock like this could well do him in.

Finding his voice again, he suggested, "So...tell me about yourself. Do you still live in London? What do you do?"

The younger man smiled, recognizing Brett was trying to bridge the gap that they were both feeling. "I'm a doctor...at last...am just finishing my residency at Sick Kids in Toronto...I'm a pediatrician."

Again Brett was flung into shock–*Sick Kids Hospital. He may have been treating our wee Merri-Lee if she had made it there.* He tried now to come back to the present, "A doctor! So I have a little brother...and he's a doctor!" He shook his head as if to loosen the cob webs.

Dr. Wall watched, recognizing the problem he had created. "I have to apologize again for my rudeness in taking you by surprise this way. I couldn't think of an easy way to...I really should have known better...but every time I come home I'm determined to meet you and then I go back to Toronto and kick myself for not having the fortitude. Thank you for receiving me...I hope we can be friends...."

he rose to go.

"I'm the one who should be apologizing. You just took me so by surprise...I've always wanted a brother...never knew I had one. Yes, we certainly can be friends." He offered his hand and the brothers shook warmly.

"Can we get together some time?"

"Absolutely, we need to get to know each other. We've already lost 22 years...let's not let any more get away on us. Do you have a time in mind?"

"I'm off to Toronto right now...then to Montreal for ten days. Can I call after that? Maybe you'd like to get together for an evening...I know Mom would love to have you for supper. She was great friends with my birth mother."

He was still sitting at his desk an hour later when Dave walked in. His emotions alternated between a wild sense of elation...he had a brother...a real live brother...a doctor no less...a real brotherly sort...and then a sense of foreboding...a memory that took him back...way...way back....

"What's the matter, Buddy? Bad news?" the younger lawyer showed his concern.

"No. No, I don't think so...quite the opposite. Did you see the young man that just left my office?"

"About an hour ago?"

"Yeah, I guess so...didn't realize it was that long."

"So this young man...what about him?"

"He's my brother," Brett's face showed a mixture of emotions, but his tone was jubilant.

"Excuse me?"

"My brother...my natural brother. Guess Mom and Dad adopted him out when he was born. Apparently Mom knew she was dying so Dr. & Mrs Wall adopted him. He's 22 and I'm 32. I was ten when Mom died. That piece of the puzzle fits."

"Well, I'll be! You really are shook up. Are you sure you should be driving to Toronto?"

"Toronto? Wow! It went right out of my mind. I should have

gone an hour ago...maybe I better call Paul and let him know what's going on with me," he reached for the phone.

"I can drive you, Buddy. You don't look like you should go it alone. I can stop over with Lee while you're busy."

Brett shook his head as he waited for the psychologist to pick up the phone. "Paul, it's Brett. I'm sorry I'm not half way to Toronto by now...just had some excitement here. Had a young man call on me...looks like he's my brother...the pieces all fit together...guess my folks adopted him out to the doctor and his wife...they knew they were both dying. Sorry I'm so incoherent...he really shook me up. Don't know if I should come today."

"Wow! That is some news! How are you feeling about this new development...besides the shock...the excitement? Do you see this as positive?"

"I do indeed! Seems like a fine young man...a doctor...name is James Wall. We'll get together in a couple of weeks when he's back from Montreal...get to know each other."

"Has it occurred to you that this might be a key to your past? Maybe the good doctor can shed some light!"

"Yeah, it came to mind...scaring me to death."

"I'll certainly be interested once you get to meet again. Meantime, you'd better just stay home this time. Don't think you should be hurrying to see me when you've got so much on your mind. Have you heard anything from Leanne since her last time in?"

"Nothing."

"Hang in there, fella'. The Lord is still in control."

CHAPTER ELEVEN

I'd best tidy the guestroom, Leanne decided. *More than a week since Dave used it...can't believe I've gotten so lax,* she mused as she stripped the bed.

The small brown envelope on the vanity caught her eye as she headed to the door with her arms full of bedding. The scrawl was familiar—*For Leanne.* "Bob, a note from Bob," she exclaimed aloud. "Dave must have left this."

Ten minutes later, with the laundry taken care of, and a cup of coffee on the desk beside her, she carefully slit the envelope, and unwrapped a small disk. "Thought you should have this, Lee. Keeping you and Brett in my prayers. Love always. Bob."

What in the world...a CD from Bob! What could he be sending me? Well, I'll just check it out right now. She slid the disk into her computer and hummed a tune as she waited for the screen to light up.

He stood with the tiny bundle in his arms, his face drenched with tears. Beside him...Dave. Then a close-up of her tiny Merri-Lee...held in Brett's two hands...her face bruised from the life-saving effort...her soft hair dark with sweat. "Oh, God," she breathed, "Where did he get these? Who could have taken these?" Her heart broke...tears ran unchecked. "O, My precious babe! Were you still alive here?" She noted every detail of her delicate features...soft dark hair, dainty wee fingers...even as she mopped at the tears that clouded her vision.

She continued scrolling. The babe was now in her little pink pyjamas, lying on the pink blanket with small white lambs–the one she had seen in her dream. "Oh, God," she cried aloud, "I can't handle this!" She rose from her chair...only to return to it again. "Who could have taken these pictures? Who would have been there?" *Bob, of course. Dave had said he came from a wedding with his camera. Yes, Bob would have taken these for me...my old childhood buddy...he would know that I'd need to see her. Brett would never had thought of it...looks like he was pretty shook up...Dave might have but...no...it would definitely be Bob.*

She saw herself...tubes...monitors...intravenous...oxygen. How horrible she looked...a lot of folk standing around her bed...heads all cut off, except for Sherry who was bending over her. She recognized Brett...Dave...Aunt Maude...Sherry's mom, Mrs. Wilson...someone in green hospital fatigues. More shots of her...taken at different angles. Brett bending over her...talking to her...or perhaps praying...looking like he'd lost ten pounds and gained ten years. His face was haggard...lack of sleep...tears.

Then...Brett holding the small white coffin. She couldn't look...couldn't go on. Again she jumped up from the chair...closing the lid on her laptop as though to close down the pain.

"Oh, God," she moaned repeatedly, "Oh, God, help me...I can't go on...I need someone." Brett's tear-streaked face flashed through her mind, "I think I need...Brett!"

The thought jolted her. *But Brett doesn't need me...doesn't want me. I know Dave would try to persuade me otherwise, but...Brett made it pretty clear....*

The phone interrupted her thoughts and she let the answering machine cut in. "Lee, it's Brett. I have some really exciting news. Can I come and see you? Please don't say 'no'."

She scooped the cordless from her desk and clicked the 'on' button. "Brett...hi." She hadn't had time to dry her tears or think what to say...she only knew she didn't want to miss him.

"Lee, sweetheart, are you okay?" His voice held both surprise and concern.

"I'm not sure...not sure at all...I...I...."

"Are you crying, Kitten?"

"Yes," she responded tearily.

"Can you tell me? Do you want to talk?"

"I...can't...not right now. I ...need some time...someone...can you come?" her voice ended in a sob.

"I'll be there as quick as I can. I'll leave right now."

Her sobs subsided...Brett would be coming. She was glad that her tenants had gone for the week-end...she would invite Brett to stay...he'd use the guest room, of course. She knew he would want to talk...probably about her discussions with Dr. Hayes. But she hadn't listened to his side of the story. *Maybe it's time I kept my promise to Dave and looked at all the evidence.* She pulled open the drawer of her desk and retrieved the cassette tapes she had brought home last week, following her session with Paul. She shivered involuntarily as she gazed at the cassettes. *Well...how bad can it be...after what I've just been through? So...what are you afraid of, Leanne? I know jolly well what I'm afraid of...afraid I won't be able to handle...to handle...his not wanting me,* she sobbed as she turned on the cassette player.

His voice was warm and friendly as they began the discussion and she noticed the progression into uncertainty as he spoke of their relationship. He faltered several times as he told of his failures as a friend and husband to her, particularly after her pregnancy began.

She listened as Dr. Hayes questioned him about his mother's pregnancies and drew parallels between his mother and herself. *I should have listened to this the first time he offered it to me,* she concluded. *How incredibly selfish I've been...wanting only to protect myself.*

The sleet on the window arrested her attention from the tape and she clicked it off. Brett would be on the road. She turned on the weather channel and listened in dismay as they warned of the impending ice storm.

"Brett...Brett...he's on the 401. I can't believe I asked him to come...I didn't know about the storm...he probably didn't either," she said aloud, as she called his cell number. She let it ring until she lost count. "He probably stopped for gas and left the phone in his brief case; I'll give him a few minutes and call again," she assured herself as she went back to the tape.

Paul had obviously raised the subject of Brett's relationship with Dave. They listened to that part of her story again, and a tearful Brett explained that their friendship...partnership was very special to him...to both of them. Dave was more than a partner...he was the brother he had never had. "But," he was quick to interject, "Lee was never a part of any business I had with Dave. Far from him wanting me for his brother-in-law, he at one time forbade me to date Lee. He was furious about the Rhonda thing and offered to resign...he would not have me playing with his sister. When he cooled down a little, he let me explain some things to him. He finally allowed me to continue to pursue Leanne...provided she approved, of course.

"As I explained to you earlier, I loved her almost from the beginning. I wouldn't admit it to myself at first, but she really moved in...."

"Moved in?"

"To my life...my heart. She just filled up all the empty spaces. I'd never been in love before...I could hardly part from her when I saw her on the week-ends. I was afraid...."

"Afraid?"

"Yeah. I was afraid she's find somebody at university...."

Why didn't I listen to these weeks ago? she admonished herself again, as she quickly touched the re-dial to call Brett's cellular. Still no answer. She tried to peer out the window in the family room but the big pane was totally iced over. "Please God, be with Brett...and with all who travel," she prayed as she turned on the news channel.

Lots of accidents in Toronto already...if folk would learn to slow down and stay at home when they don't need to be out....

She tried again and let it ring and ring and ring. Suddenly, her heart jumped as she heard a click. "Hello." It sounded strange and far away.

"Hello. This is Leanne. Is this you, Brett?"

"No, Ma'am. This isn't Brett. There's been an accident...I just heard this phone ringing and ringing and finally realized it was in the briefcase on the shoulder of the highway, so I picked it up and answered."

"Oh, God, no...no...no...please no."

"I'm sorry, Ma'am."

"Can you tell me anything about the accident...if he's okay?"

"I'm real sorry. I can't see too much. The police have stopped all east-bound traffic and it's hard to see through the blowing snow. There's about three vehicles or so...one's upside down in the ditch...a big SUV is on it's side, and a pickup truck...I think it is...."

"Can you see what the overturned vehicle is like?" She was almost screaming...trying desperately to control her hysteria.

"Not really, Ma'am, it's nearly covered with snow. Could be a BMW judging from the back-end...tail lights. The rest of it is pretty well...." He stopped suddenly, wondering to whom he was giving all this information. "Who am I talking to, Ma'am?"

"I'm sorry," she sobbed. "I'm Brett's wife."

"I guess I shouldn't be getting you so upset, Ma'am. I'm not sure there is a Brett involved here," he tried to comfort her, forgetting that he was using Brett's phone.

She apprised him of the fact. Could he tell her of their whereabouts on the highway? Brett couldn't have gotten far.

"We're still in London, Ma'am...just past the intersection of Wellington on the 401...you know where that is?" She nodded, forgetting he couldn't see her. "Well, it looks to me like a vehicle must have lost control...here comes the ambulance, now...guess we should be able to tell pretty soon if there's anybody alive...." he stopped as she gasped...suddenly aware that he had said too much. "Maybe you could call again, Ma'am. Give it a few minutes and I might know more. Maybe I can help here...."

"Yes, okay, I will. And will you please retrieve Brett's briefcase and make sure the police get it?"

She went back to the news channel and fearfully watched the snowy scene unfolding. The remains of the car had been turned upright and a number of men were working feverishly to extricate the driver, who was obviously...."Oh, God...I'm not sure I can watch. I know You are watching...please...please...." she sobbed, as she watched in horror. "Oh God, I haven't asked a lot in the last six months...I haven't even talked to you all that much. Forgive my failing...Oh, Lord, I can't face this loss without You."

The reporter continued his commentary. They were using the jaws of life and the driver of the BMW.... She paced endlessly...unwilling to watch...unable to take her eyes from the scene, and as she paced she murmured, "Oh, God! Oh, God! Oh, God!"

She watched as they lifted him from the wreckage, placed him on a stretcher and worked over him...some sort of life supports, she decided. That must mean there is still life. He was too far away...it was too dark...too much snow...she couldn't see who it was...a big man, obviously. *It must be Brett! How could his briefcase be on the road?* The ambulance drove away and she sat stricken...desperately alone...*but not alone,* she reminded herself. *God is right here with me..* It finally occurred to her that she needed to call Dave.

Aunt Maude answered the phone and an anxious Leanne asked if Dave was there. "I'll get him at once," Aunt Maude recognized the stress in Lee's voice.

He's at Aunt Maude's. Guess he must have placed his phone on 'call forward' before they went for supper.

"Lee...hi, sugar bug. Nice to have you call big brother...even if you are interupting an incredible supper." Her sniffle put his mind on alert. "What's up?"

"Dave...I think Brett...Brett...he's been in an accident. He was coming to see me and...and...we didn't know about the storm...and...."

"Take it easy, Sis. He's probably okay. Why do you think he's been in an accident? He may be travelling slowly...."

"No...no...no..." she cried. "Someone else answered his cell phone. They found it beside the road...in his briefcase."

"Lee baby, listen to me. His briefcase could have dropped out when he stopped...someone could have stolen...."

"No," she shrieked. "He's been in an accident. I think someone ran into him." She paused, realizing she didn't really make sense. "Turn on the news channel...the accident is right there...in London...on the 401...the ambulance has taken him away...." she tried to explain between sobs...her confused thoughts supplying only fragmented bits of information.

Still carrying the cordless phone, Dave flicked on the news channel. There had indeed been an accident! They gathered around the television...watching spellbound as police directed traffic, ambulances stood waiting. All east-bound lanes were blocked and traffic backed up. Reporters milled about.

"You're right, Lee, there certainly has been an accident. You think Brett was involved and that they have taken him...somewhere?"

"Yes...yes...I think that's his BMW...over on the right...can't see it too good...it was upside down and they turned it back...I'm sure those are his tail lights."

"That could well be. Give us a little time here and we'll get in touch once we find out if that's him...and where he is." Then, quickly he added, "Lee, you can't come–you know that! You can't come–not in this storm! You'll need to...."

"Don't tell me that, Dave! How can I *not* come? He could die...he could...."

"Stop it, Leanne! You can't stop him from dying...and you won't get out of the city in this storm. You need to stay home...and pray...and we will find him and keep you posted. Are you listening?"

"Not really," she admitted through her tears.

"Lee, honey, I'm glad you want to be with Brett, but if he's injured...he'll be in a trauma unit...being operated on...or...only God knows. Please try to get your mind around this...bypass your emotions. Will you do that, Lee? I'll call as soon as I know something, okay?"

"Fine," she managed shakily.

She noticed her hand shaking as she sat holding the phone, not wanting to put it down. Somehow it represented a lifeline to Brett...to her family. "Silly," she told herself. "They're not any closer if I put it down...I must be in shock." She called Brett's cellular and was informed that the customer she had dialed was not standing by. She wondered where the phone was now...*did the police have it? ...did the man on the side of the road keep it?...and what happened to his briefcase?* She wondered what he might have in it, and if it would be of value...legal importance or... *Horrors! I'm acting like he's already gone...guess I've worked in estates too long...I'm acting like a lawyer,* she moaned.

She made her way to the bedroom and sank on her knees by the bed. "Oh, God," she prayed aloud, "Forgive me for letting *self* control me this past year...for my self-protective behaviour–cutting Brett out of my life...avoiding my family. Oh, God, I need them all so much! I need You in control of my life again...I give it back to you now. Make of me whatever you want. And Lord..." she paused as her emotions overcame her resolve, then tearfully, she continued, "Lord...I once again give up my claim to Brett...to his life or death...I know he belongs to You...and I take my hands off him...but dear Lord...you know how much I want him back!"

When the tears subsided, she rose and washed her face. *My time can be better spent than crying,* she decided. *I'll just finish up here and get ready to leave for London as soon as this storm is out of the way.* Her eyes strayed to the phone and she decided to replay the messages on her answering machine...just to hear his voice once more....

"Lee, it's Brett. I have some really exciting news. Can I come and see you? Please don't say 'no'." Tears overwhelmed her. *I thought I was done with that,* she wiped at them disgustedly. She played it again. *So Brett was coming to see me...he wanted to come...he had some exciting news...he wasn't coming just because I asked him.* The information she had missed before, now gave her a small comfort...eased a portion of the mountain of guilt she was feeling for bringing him out in a storm...maybe causing his death....

"Leanne, it's Dave. You were right...it is Brett's car. They have taken him to University Hospital. Uncle Ben and I are on our way there now...streets are heavy...visibility almost non existent...make sure you stay in until this is over and the roads cleared," his voice crackled and she strained to hear.

Then impatiently, "Do you know anything about him? How badly he was hurt...if he's still alive?"

"Sorry, honey. He must have been alive at the scene...the

ambulance took him...we won't know anything else till we get there...if we get there. You can pray for us, too, and for everybody out here."

"I tried to call his cell. I guess they've shut it off."

"We tried, too. I hope the police have it, and not the guy who found it . I'll call again."

"Dave...what about permission...you know...in case he needs to be operated...or...?"

"I'll see to it, Lee."

CHAPTER TWELVE

I should probably eat something...guess I've had enough coffee...I'll be awake for a week...maybe I'll need to be awake for a week. She collapsed wearily on the sofa and shut off the television. *I've seen enough of that to traumatize me for a week, too,* she decided. She prayed again for Brett...the doctors tending him...Dave and Sherry and wee Mandy...the Wilsons...Bob ...Uncle Ben...Aunt Maude...her thoughts drifted away....

She woke shielding her eyes from the blinding light–the sun had just broken through the heavy cloud cover. *Where am I? ...the sofa...I spent the night on the sofa...I never went to bed. Ten o'clock...and I didn't get ready to leave for London. Got to call Bill and Billie and let them know about Brett. Funny Dave never called back. Better call him first.*

The blinking light caught her attention as she reached for the phone. She pressed the button and Dave's voice caught her by surprise. "Leanne, I hope you haven't started out in this terrible mess. If you're at home give me a call. It's 10 p.m."

She dialed him quickly. "Sorry, Dave. I fell asleep on the couch. Can't believe I didn't hear the phone. Guess I was more exhausted than I thought. So, tell me...."

"I'm glad you're still there, honey bug. We nearly went bonkers when we couldn't raise you on either phone. Brett has some rather serious injuries...damaged kidney...broken hip...I don't know if that's all. We didn't get to see him last night...he was in emergency surgery for hours...Of course he's unconscious. I didn't get to talk to the doctors...the staff didn't know or wouldn't tell me anything...especially since I wasn't his wife...." he tried to joke.

"So they would tell me?"

"You can certainly give them a call. Ben and I will be going...."

She didn't hear the rest of it as her mind flew into gear. She would be on her way within the hour. No need to alarm Dave. She flipped to the weather channel. The storm seemed to be over, but the roads were heavy...travel not advised. Still high winds. They proceeded to list closures on the 400...407...401. A pile-up near Kitchener...she could swing off there and take Number Seven Highway, then on to Number Four. She would make it. She would travel carefully...she was a good driver...had a good sleep.

"Dave," she finally interjected, "Do they know what happened?"

"Not sure. It looks like the big sport utility vehicle must have slammed into him...travelling too fast. Don't know about the pick-up...anything can happen in those conditions. A few minor fender benders down the line as vehicles tried to stop. Nothing as serious as this."

"Anybody else injured?"

"I'm sure there are. Nobody wanted to satisfy my curiosity."

She called Bill and asked for prayer for Brett, left a note for Ian and Liz, before she quickly shovelled a path in her driveway. She paused before backing out the purple Lexus and murmured, "Thank you, God, for keeping Brett alive...for this car...that it works so well...that it's new...that my tank is full...." She continued giving thanks as she slowly made her way through heavy streets to the 401.

It was three o'clock before she finally presented her case to the nurse in charge. "So you are Mrs. Walker? I'm sure you can see him...he is still unconscious, you know. The doctor will be in within the hour...a lot of accidents last night." she indicated his room on their way down the hall.

He was alone in the room...unless the jumble of intravenous tubes, monitors, bandages and oxygen paraphernalia could be considered company. Leanne moved closer; was it really him? His head was completely swathed in bandages...his face blackened–maybe the air bag didn't work...or maybe it did–her inspection continued...one leg suspended in a cast...heart monitor on his chest...blood-pressure cuff on one arm...cast on the other...a neck brace...a tube coming out of his nose. She shuddered. *This is just too close to home...even worse than I had!*

She sat down on the wooden chair, and laid her face on the bed near him. "Dear Lord Jesus, it's me again...Leanne. Thank you that Brett is still with us...and thank you for getting me here safely...it was quite a trip, Lord! Please...don't let him have brain damage," she paused as tears escaped, "and please don't let him have a broken neck...Oh, God, he...I...couldn't bear it." Again she paused to consider what either of those might mean in their marriage...their lives. She could look after an invalid...after all she had cared for her dad for over a year...but brain damage? What if he didn't know her? Or what if he was a paraplegic? She wiped her tears again, then continued, "But, Lord, as I said last night...he's your child...he's in your hands, and.... " a fresh burst of tears, then, "I'll accept him and love him...and care for him whatever condition...."

"Hello, there. You must be Mrs. Walker. They told me you had come. I'm Dr. Longo...from neurology. You look like you have questions?"

"Yes, doctor, yes, I do. Tell me about the bandages on his head...his brain...." she paused, not knowing exactly what to ask.

"I'm responsible for the bandages. He has quite a gash...and yes, he has lost all of his hair. Scan shows some swelling of the blood vessels...he took quite a hit...looks like it came from the left side...caught him...."

"Tell me what effect that will have on his brain," she cut in. "Is that considered damage? Will it be permanent?"

"Whoa! Hold on, little lady! We don't know for sure, but this kind of swelling often goes down and the brain resumes its normal functions. His memory may be affected...he may not remember who he is...family...friends. We can't predict with certainty...." he stopped at the look of anguish on her face.

"Do you know anything about...his neck ...his....?

"I can tell you it isn't broken...some badly cracked vertebrae. He isn't paralyzed if that's what you want to know. It will be a while before he'll have to worry about that. I can't comment on the rest of his injuries...not my department." He perused the chart, checked the blood-pressure monitor, then lifted the patient's eyelids before he turned again to Leanne, "He's a very lucky man...he's alive! I'll keep tabs on him...let you know if there's any change."

If there's any change, not *when* she noted, as the door closed behind him.

I think I'll slip outside and call Dave on my cell...easier than finding a payphone, she decided and headed to the elevator.

"Look who we have here!" the booming voice of Uncle Ben, as he stepped off the elevator with Dave at his side. "And how did you get here?"

"And what are you doing here?" from Dave. "Didn't I tell you...?"

She grinned as he stopped...then grabbed her in a bear hug. "I got here around three o'clock...roads were really heavy...401 was closed at Cambridge...Kitchener...so I just took an alternate. Took me twice as long as it should have...but...the Lord looked after me."

"Have you seen Brett?"

"Yes. Come." She led the way to his room, where they stood speechless. "The neurologist was in...Dr. Longo, I believe. Says his head took quite a hit...some swelling there...it could go away and leave him normal...." she paused as her voice broke, "and...his neck isn't broken...cracked vertebrae." Dave slipped his arms around her and let her sob into his shoulder.

Uncle Ben Davis cleared his throat, then moved closer to the bed. "Is there any part of him that didn't get...?"

"Dr. Longo doesn't know what else...it's not his department. Not hard to guess...looks like an arm and a leg...all those tubes down his nose...throat...must be some internal...." another burst of tears as she reached for a tissue.

"Are you family?" the nurse asked as she came through the door. Mr. Walker is hardly out of surgery...you may want to come back another time...." she proceeded to check his vitals and update the chart.

"Yes," Lee and Dave spoke in unison. "Would it be possible to see the doctors...whoever treated him...operated on him?" Dave asked.

"They may be in to check on him in the next hour or so. I believe Dr. Andrews operated on him in the early hours of the morning...you may wish to leave a message for him...he's a busy man."

"Can you tell us what the operation was for?"

"I think you'd best discuss these matters with the doctor in charge...." she paused as two medics in green fatigues joined them.

"Hello, I'm Dr. Andrews...my colleague Dr. Barth. I take it you are family?" They nodded as he proceeded. "You are indeed fortunate...."

"I'm Mrs. Walker. Can you tell me what all of this represents? I understand he was operated; can you tell me for what?"

"Indeed I can! I removed your husband's left kidney...it was badly damaged. That's why—or at least one of the reasons—for the tube in his nose...we must keep his digestive system clear. His left hip was shattered...his left arm broken...though not as badly as it might've been. It goes without saying that his ribs are badly broken in the back...cracked in front...his left lung punctured...."

They stood stunned...not knowing what to ask...yet wanting to know the prognosis.

"So," Ben began, "what...what do you see...?"

"He's a strong man...strong body...healthy...that will bode well for him. When he regains consciousness...he'll need a reason to live."

Leanne whimpered and Dave again put his arm around her. "He'll have that," she assured the doctor.

"I'm sure...I'm sure," he smiled.

CHAPTER THIRTEEN

"Seven days! It's been seven whole days, and he hasn't moved," Leanne sobbed to Sherry as they sat over lunch.

"I know, Lee," her sister in law's voice was sympathetic. "But you know what kind of pain he'll be in when he wakes...I know it's hard but...maybe...maybe the Lord is giving his body a chance to heal...while he can't feel it...you know...?" she finished weakly. Lee nodded as Sherry continued, "Do you intend to stay with him...in his room...until he regains consciousness?"

"Yes, I'd like to...if they let me. When I came I thought it would be nice for him to wake and find me here...but after they told me he may not know me...or himself for that matter... I told the Lord I'd be there anyway...to care for him...whatever his state of mind or health. I'll need His grace though."

"So what about your studies, Lee? Aren't you missing a lot of classes?"

"Not a lot. My classes are scheduled two days a week...the rest is independent research ...papers...ad infinitum. I can do most of it here. I talked to the dean on Monday...think I can get the classes by e-mail. They've certainly been co-operative...have treated me very well. Guess they know I'd have to drop out otherwise...I can't go back to school with Brett...." she stopped as her voice broke.

Sherry smiled, "I'm so glad you're back, Lee. I've missed you so terribly...and Dave...he can hardly pray without tears. They've missed you at the office, too."

"Speaking of the office, how are they getting on there? Do they have enough staff?"

Sherry was already shaking her head. "The guys both put in gobs of overtime...Dave works three or four nights every week...sometimes he brings it home. I think Brett worked every day but Sunday, and most nights. Course he took Friday afternoons off to go to Toronto to see the psychologist."

"They've never mentioned anything to me about it...not even Dave."

"Brett wouldn't let him. He didn't want you to come back under pressure. They really need another lawyer...they're both doing a lot of corporate work...they can't keep up. Dave thinks they could use another lawyer...even if you came back."

"And now Brett will be out of it for a while. Maybe I can do something to help...once he regains consciousness, I mean. Poor Dave...he'll be scrambling to please clients...too bad we couldn't get someone on a temporary basis who knows something about corporate law," she mused.

Sherry smirked. "I know just the man–how about Bob?"

"Bob? Your brother? Is he available? I thought he was all tied up at Kingston?"

"Not so. Dave would have brought him in long ago, but Brett...."

"Brett didn't want him?"

"He didn't want anybody replacing you. Didn't want you to feel either displaced or obligated to come back. The man loves you, Lee. He didn't want to do anything that might offend you or...." she shrugged.

"Bless his heart. If I could have believed he loved me months ago, none of this would have happened. I've sure struggled with the dream thing. Dr. Hayes finally convinced me that it really did cause the change in his personality...his behaviour. Guess I'm afraid of...what he might be like when he wakes...if he wakes!" She was in tears again. "Dave and I need to talk about this...we need to do something to get help for him...it will have to be temporary until Brett...until he can make decisions again," she finished.

CHAPTER FOURTEEN

The activity around his bed frightened her. She stopped inside the door. The oxygen apparatus had been removed...the leg harness...gone.... She watched in terror as a technician took off the heart monitor. "Oh, God...no!" she cried, "no...please...no...don't let him be gone!"

They looked up in surprise. "No need to worry, Mrs. Walker," the doctor smiled. "He's doing very well...we're just making him a little more comfortable. His recovery is really quite remarkable. We should see some signs of consciousness pretty soon."

As the door closed behind them, she sank wearily on the chair...laid her head on his bed...and wept. "Thank you, God...thank you." She noted that the bandage had been removed from his head and replaced with a long strip along the left side and back. They weren't kidding when they said they'd shaved his hair. I better get him a toque...his head will be cold. At least the swelling is going down on his face...he looks a little more like Brett.

A thrill ran through her...did his eyelid really flutter as she gently kissed his swollen cheek? She stood spellbound...afraid to look away in case it happened again. Must have been my overly-active desire, she decided. It happened again. *It happened again...it did...I know it did this time! He's coming around!*

She was still standing beside the bed when the nurse came in an hour later. *Shall I tell her?* she wondered. "His eyelids fluttered twice about an hour ago," she ventured.

"I guess that could be possible," the nurse answered nonchalantly as she went about checking his vitals and marking the chart. "Don't get so anxious...it could be a while yet." With that she was gone.

I think I'll slip out to the car and call Dr. Hayes...let him know about this...ask him what I can expect when Brett wakes. Sure wish I could use my cellular in here.

"You're in luck...he had a cancellation today," the receptionist replied as she transferred the call.

"Leanne, hello, how has your week gone?"

Suddenly she felt like sobbing her heart out...then bit her trembling lip and tried to explain what had happened to Brett. He listened attentively, encouraging her when she stopped to wipe her tears and blow her nose. "So...that's why he wasn't there on Friday. I'm sorry I didn't think to call sooner," she finished.

"Can I ask where you are, Leanne? Are you here in Toronto?"

"No, I'm at the hospital in London...University Hospital. They brought Brett here after the accident...and...."

"How did you get there, Leanne?"

"I drove...but not till Saturday...the storm was over...."

"But the roads were impassable?"

"Just some of them. I took a couple smaller highways."

He paused, trying to get a picture of this new development. Leanne had driven to London in near impossible conditions to be with Brett. A few weeks ago, she wouldn't commit to listening to his session on tape. Something had obviously happened. *Thank you, Lord for the change of heart,* he prayed...then wondered how he might approach the subject without causing her more pain than she was feeling at this moment.

She saved him the uncertainty. "Brett was coming to see me...he was excited about something and wanted to share it with me. I...I...had gotten some pictures of our baby from our friend, Bob, and they broke my heart. Brett...and the family were all there weeping...Brett holding wee Merri-Lee...and then...and then...."

"And then?" he prompted.

"And then I knew that Brett and I needed each other...and the phone rang...and it was him! Neither of us had heard about the storm...he shouldn't have started out when he saw it was so bad. I didn't even notice until the ice crystals hit the big window...." She struggled to regain her composure. "And now...and now...."

"Take it easy, Lee...just stop when you need to. And now...what?"

"Brett has a brain injury. The doctor thinks he'll be okay when the swelling goes down but his memory may be affected for a while...he may not know me...or himself...or anybody else. Can you tell me what to expect? And how long?"

"I'm not sure I can, Lee, but I can give you some possibilities. He may well need time to recover all of his memory bank. That doesn't mean he'll be illiterate or deaf and dumb. He may not know who he is...he may revert back to his childhood or teen years...depending on where the swelling is. He may remember friends from back then...look for his parents. Since you weren't a part of those years.... Do you get what I mean? He may not know you for some time."

"So, how do I respond to that? Should I tell him who he is...who I am?"

"Who he is will be okay. Who you are? I wouldn't advise that...depending on how old he thinks he is...if he's back in his early teens...he either won't believe you're his wife...or he'll be terrified. I'd let him remember at his own pace...though, of course, there's no need to hide family photographs...keep friends at bay...."

"What about the office? Should I take him there?"

"When he becomes curious about who he is...what he does...yes, I would say he should go there. Familiar places...familiar faces...familiar foods...familiar activities...they all play a part in jogging the memory. Don't push it...just let it happen."

"I appreciate that Dr. Paul. I'll be staying with him as much as I can. They've let me stay overnight so far. I'm sure I saw his eyelids flutter twice today...the nurse wasn't so sure, but I'm excited anyway. It can't be too soon for me."

"Let me know how he's doing from time to time, Leanne. I'd like to work in a trip to see him when he regains consciousness."

CHAPTER FIFTEEN

He handed her the casserole dish with ham and scalped potatoes. "Sherry thought you should have a reprieve from struggling to find something gluten-free in the cafeteria." he commented with a smile.

"Oh, Dave. I'm so glad you've come. I think Brett's beginning to come around. I'm sure he's moved his lips and eyelids a time or two, or else I'm seeing things. I hope I'll be here when he opens his eyes. Dr. Hayes doesn't think he'll know us for a while...until his memory bank opens up...or whatever."

"Can't be too soon, for me; the Hencken bail hearing is coming up in a couple of weeks. I was really counting on him to head it up. Are you still game?"

"You bet I am. It'll be hard to leave Brett...especially if he's still comatose. I'm asking for a miracle!"

"Me, too. Sherry mentioned that you discussed having Bob come and work with me while I'm waiting on Brett. How do you think he'll respond once he knows what's going on? Do you think he'll feel betrayed...replaced...undermined?"

She nodded. "Maybe all of the above...but it can't be helped. We can't let you continue to exhaust yourself; somebody has to take charge. Once he comes to himself, I think he'll be glad that you took steps to ensure the integrity of the practice Wish I could help. Actually, I'm all caught up with my studies. Loads of time in here. You could send me something I can work on...keep me happy...productive...fulfilled," she grinned.

"Sounds like my partner in crime...er...law," he returned her grin.

They both jumped as the intravenous tubes moved slightly. His eyelids lifted almost imperceptibly and his lips moved. They moved closer. Lee took his hand. "Brett, can you hear us? It's me, Leanne, and Dave."

His eyes opened, unseeing. His lips moved.

"Call the nurse," she suggested.

As Dave headed for the door it opened and Dr. Longo stepped in, accompanied by the nurse in charge. "I hear there's been some movement," he began, as Leanne looked in surprise at the nurse.

Guess she took me more seriously than she let on, she concluded.

A groan escaped the patient as the neurologist lifted the eyelid. "He certainly is coming around...won't be long now." Then turning to the hefty matron, he asked, "Will you be able to keep an eye here...I'll be back once I finish my rounds."

Dave turned to Leanne as the door closed, "I guess I should be getting back to the office, but I sure hate to leave you here alone all the time...and I'd love to be here when Brett wakens. Will you let me know when it happens?"

"I'll do my best. It may not happen all at once...maybe by degrees...wish I could use my cellular in here...inconvenient to run to the car and use it...or find a payphone. I hate to leave Brett–like you, I'd love to be here when he wakens."

As if he heard them speak, his eyes opened slightly. They watched spellbound, as he tried to focus, then grimaced and closed his eyes. "Brett...are you awake? It's Leanne...and Dave."

He moaned as he tried to shake off the heavy fog that bound him. His eyes fluttered open again...and again he grimaced and closed them

"Are you in pain?" Lee asked as she tried to get him to focus. As though waking was too much effort, he slipped back into unconsciousness.

"Oh, Dave," she said as tears ran freely, "I want so much to have him back...all of him."

He nodded, and taking her hand, prayed for God's very best for his sister and her husband, who just happened to be his good friend, partner, and brother-in-law.

"Thank Sherry for the neat lunch...like an oasis in the desert," she smiled as he gave her a hug before he left for the office.

Leanne tried to concentrate on her reading material...but between visits from the nurse and her constant watch over Brett, she absorbed little of value. She glanced as her watch as the supper wagons rolled down the hall. *Guess I should eat my apple and the goodies Sherry sent. Won't need much more after that great lunch. Won't have to leave right now either when Brett....* She stopped short of promising herself that he could wake up any minute. *Tomorrow will be nine days since this nightmare began...can't imagine what I'll do if he doesn't....* Again she paused, hesitating to go there.

She slept fitfully on her small cot...her ears attuned to any movement from the man in the bed.

CHAPTER SIXTEEN

Good thing I got up early, she congratulated herself, as she heard the doctors on their morning rounds.

"Good morning, Dr. Andrews."

He muttered a hurried "Good morning," picked up the chart and turned to the nurse, "So, he's showing signs of coming around. Looks good here...maybe we can remove...." his voice muffled as he pulled the curtain, "...looks like the right kidney is functioning well...of course the catheters will need to stay in for a while yet."

In response to Leanne's anxious look, he stopped at the door, "He's doing good...better than expected." Then he was gone. She waited while the nurse busied herself behind the curtain, and when at length it opened, she noticed that the tube down his nose had been removed.

"Thank you, Lord," she whispered as she planted a small kiss on his bruised face. Then addressing her special man, "You really are starting to look just the littlest bit like Brett."

She had settled into reading when she felt his eyes on her. She looked up startled, "You're awake!"

His lips moved as though in response but no sound came. He continued to watch as she moved closer, touched his hand. *I hope Dr. Longo is making his rounds...if I leave to call someone...he may be gone again when we arrive.* She spoke in quiet soothing tones, wildly happy...yet wondering...was he lucid?...could he understand?...did he know her? "Do you know where you are?" she ventured.

He attempted to move his head but the restraining device held him fast. *Looks like he was trying to indicate 'no,'* she decided.. She tried again, "You're in the hospital...you've been in an accident. Do you understand?" This wasn't working. "If you understand, can you blink your eyes twice?" He did so. She restrained herself from screaming out her joy. *He's alive! His brain is working! Thank you, God!*

"Can you talk?" His lips moved but made no sound. "Do you need some water?" He blinked twice. "I'll see if you're allowed." She ran for the nurse and they both returned. The nurse held the straw to his mouth and he slowly sipped the precious liquid. *No wonder he can't talk...ten days without a drink.....*

"I'll try to locate Dr. Longo," the nurse stated matter-of-factly, "he should be on the floor by now."

Lee ran for the payphone in the lounge. Thankfully it wasn't in use. "Dave...Dave," she cried excitedly, "he's awake and his brain seems to be functioning!"

In reply to his question, she added, "No, he can't talk yet, but he can blink if I ask him something. I want to get back.... Come when you can." and she was gone.

It seemed oniy minutes before Dave walked in. "Does he know you, Lee?" he asked as he stood by the bed.

She shook her head. "I don't think so." Then motioning him to the other side of the room, she whispered the instructions and suggestions from Dr. Hayes. "He doesn't think it a good idea to tell Brett I'm his wife. If he can't remember beyond his teen years...he'll find it impossible to believe he's married. He suggested we let him remember on his own."

"Wow! How are you with that?"

"I was pretty devastated at first but I can certainly see the wisdom in it. Don't know how I'll feel about having a big kid or a teenager instead of a husband...but God still knows the way through the wilderness...and I promised Him I would accept whatever...." she stopped as tears threatened her voice.

"You've had quite a year...little sis," he slipped a comforting arm around her as they returned to the patient.

Brett opened his eyes as he heard them approach, and his gaze followed their movements.

"Hi, there, fella," Dave began. "Do you know who we are?"

"Will you blink for us...twice for 'yes'...once for 'no'? Do you understand?" she asked.

He blinked twice. "Thank you. Now can you tell us...do you know us?"

He blinked only once. They looked at each other.

"Are you in pain?"

Again one blink.

"Have you lost your voice?"

His lips moved...he blinked twice.

"I want to stay here and look after you. Is that okay with you?"

His eyes closed twice and remained closed.

"I think we've tired him out. Better let him rest," she suggested. They moved to the end of the room to enjoy the coffee Dave had picked up on his way over.

"I wish I could talk to a doctor who knows everything going on here...instead of just bits and pieces...you know...the urologist looks after his kidney, or lack of it...the neurologist looks after his brain and stuff...the orthopaedic surgeon...his hip and arm? What about his voice box? What about his punctured lung...is there a lungologist? Or who looks after these other parts that are injured? Do you know what I mean? I'd love to get the whole picture."

"Yeah, I'm with you. It's plenty frustrating ...but maybe we know all we need to for now. When the time is right, we'll know."

CHAPTER SEVENTEEN

"I'm Reverend Bill Somerville, and I'd like to see Brett Walker," Leanne heard his exchange with the nurse and hurried to the door.

"Pastor Somerville, how good to see you...I was hoping you'd stop by...I heard you were back...it's been so long...."

"So it has...way too long!" He offered his hand.

"So how was Haiti? Did the extension get underway at the orphanage?"

"Oh, yes. Well underway. Amazing what those matrons have made do with. They'll now have a larger dining room, play room and laundry room." Then turning to Leanne, he asked, "So how have you been, Leanne?"

"Well...I have to say that the Lord has been with me even though I haven't really...haven't really...."

"Realized it?"

"Yes. Or deserved it. Guess I've been too distraught at times to acknowledge that He's there...maybe even angry at Him for allowing...."

"You have certainly struggled this past year...we have kept you in our prayers. So...how is our patient doing?"

"Doctors say he is doing well...better than expected."

"And Leanne says?"

She grinned. "Leanne says it's not nearly good enough...after ten days, I mean. He's trying to talk from time to time...can indicate 'yes' and 'no' by moving his head...now that the apparatus has been removed. He doesn't know who he is...or who we are. They think it will all come back at some point. Can't be too soon for me."

"Or Dave, either, I would imagine. Who's minding the store?"

"Well, so far just Dave, but Sherry's brother Bob is coming the first of the week."

"Wonderful that he's available. The Lord must surely have his hand in that."

"I'm sure. And Dave and Bob are such good buddies...studied together for years...know how to get along...work together...they'll do well."

They both jumped at the sudden movement in the bed. Brett opened his eyes. "Hello," he managed in a raspy voice.

"Hello, you're awake?" she responded.

He nodded.

"Hello, Brett. I'm Pastor Bill Somerville. Remember me?"

He shook his head and closed his eyes, as if in confusion.

She motioned the pastor to the hallway and continued in low tones, "He seems quite overwhelmed with all of the folk who know him. He's not sure who he is at this point. Dr. Hayes–he's the psychologist–thinks he'll regain his memory...maybe over a period of time. He took a pretty bad blow to the head."

"How are his other injuries coming along? I understand he lost a kidney?"

"Yes, he did. All seems to be well so far...no complications. His arm is doing well, and the hip is healing nicely. I expect they'll have him out of bed before long. Once he can get around...with a walker...he'll be able to go home."

"Is that positive? Will you be able to care for him, or will you need help?"

"I don't have any answers for those questions. It will depend on what kind of shape he's in and how much memory...you know what I mean?...if he can care for some of his needs himself...or if he'll be helpless...."

"That would be a challenge. How about your classes, Leanne?"

"Well, of course, Brett's needs will have to come first. Right now I'm keeping up my classes by e-mail and doing some work for Dave. Course I'm not doing anything else except sitting here with Brett.

Once he can make himself understood, I may go home at night...I'd get better rest."

"You don't think you can leave him?"

"I don't want to. I'm the one constant in his jumbled world. He knows my name and looks for me when he wakes. Course he doesn't know who I am, but I'm a familiar face...everyone else keeps changing with the shifts. He doesn't know old friends...not even Dave and Sherry. Ben and Maude Davis have been up...." she shook her head.

"How are you coping with that, Leanne...with his not knowing you?"

"I'm devastated. But he doesn't know himself, either. I'm prepared to wait for the Lord on this; He's with us and He knows the end from the beginning. It's a good time for me to contemplate my life with Brett...both past and future...."

"You're quite a girl, Leanne. Let me pray for you before I go," and taking her hands in his he asked the Lord to sustain them both, and for–what seemed to Leanne like a miracle–total healing of Brett's mind and body.

CHAPTER EIGHTEEN

"The doctor would like you to try to sit up, Brett," she explained as she slowly began to bring up the head of the bed. "Does that feel okay?" she asked.

"Yes," he surprised her.

"Would you like to try sitting in a chair sometime soon?"

He nodded. "I'd like to walk."

"Not today," she assured him.

"Why?"

"Because you're still pretty weak. Maybe I could take you in a wheelchair. Would that ...?" She stopped as he shook his head.

"I want to walk."

"I'll ask the doctor...perhaps he'll leave an order with the nurse. Okay?"

He nodded.

She returned with an orderly. "You can't walk today. You'll need to practise sitting first. Come, let us help you."

He struggled to sit up, his face showing the strain, then fell back, exhausted. "I can't," he whispered. "I can't."

"It's all right, Brett...it's okay. We'll take it slow and try again another time. I think we need to crank up your bed so you can sit a little straighter." She wiped the sweat from his forehead and smoothed the new growth that was beginning to look like hair. *He's looking more and more like my Brett...pretty soon he'll be back,* she reassured herself with a smile.

She straightened his bed and folded back the spread. "Would you like to talk to me?" she asked, noticing he was watching her movements.

He nodded.

"Can you tell me..." she paused wondering what to ask that he would know the answer to. "Can you tell me what you like to eat?"

He looked questioningly at her.

"Do you like meat and vegetables...fruit?"

"Yes."

"What kind of meat? Do you like roast beef...steak...pork chops?"

He nodded.

Guess I need to ask him something that he can't answer with 'yes' or 'no'. Let me see. "What is your favourite food...for supper?"

"Chinese food."

Yippee. We scored on that one. He hasn't lost everything. "Where do you get Chinese food? Do you buy it? Or go to a restaurant?"

"I don't know," his eyes looked through her...vacant...seeing...but not seeing.

O God, help! I can't watch him struggle..

"Well hi there, sugar bug," he said as he swung through the door.

"Hi, yourself, big brother. Come on in. Brett and I were just having a talk."

"Hello, Brett. Remember me? I was here yesterday."

Brett nodded. "Dave."

"Brett was just telling me his favourite food is Chinese."

"How about that! Why don't I get some and we'll enjoy it together? Would you like that?"

Brett grinned. "Sounds good."

That's one of his old expressions. Praise the Lord!...and that grin....

"So what kind shall I get?" He looked from Leanne to Brett.

"What would you like, Brett?" She noticed that again his eyes looked vacant as though struggling to bring it up on his mental screen. Turning to Dave, she said, "I think he likes almond chicken...beef chow mein...maybe some fried rice...and, oh yes...some ribs...honey garlic ribs."

"Okay," she said as Dave left, "Why don't you ask me some

questions. Would you like to do that?"

He nodded. "Are you a nurse?"

She paused, wondering how best to answer. "No, I'm not a nurse."

"Who are you?"

"I'm Leanne Stevenson."

"Why are you here?"

"I came to take care of you after your accident."

It seemed to satisfy him for a moment or two, then he asked again, "Why?"

"Because I know you and...I'm concerned that you get good care."

"Why do you know me?"

"Because we worked together?"

"What did we do? What kind of work?"

"We're both lawyers."

"I'm a lawyer?"

"Yes."

"Is Dave a lawyer?"

"Yes. We all work together. I think maybe you should rest for a few minutes until he gets back. You'll need to sit up again... We'll talk more another time."

He lay on the partially-raised bed, his face white with the effort he had expended. He still wore the puzzled expression.

The wheels are certainly going around in there, she observed as she sat by his bed. *I wonder if he'll be able to eat any of the Chinese food...sure hope so...bet Dave thought it might jog some memory. At least he seems to know he's an adult...how horrible if he re-lived his painful childhood.*

He struggled to sit up as Dave arrived, bringing tantalizing aromas in small cartons.

"Are you hungry?" Leanne asked, as she turned up the bed and helped him to sit..

"I am now," he smiled.

Sure does sound like my Brett. She smiled in return. "Well, let's just see if you like any of this."

"I like any kind of Chinese food," he countered, then bowed his

93

head as they asked the Lord's blessing.

Funny, she thought, the way his memory is so selective. He remembers a lot of 'stuff' but can't seem to recall the most important of all...family...relationships. Wonder if he remembers a relationship with God. I'll talk to him about that sometime soon, she decided.

Dave talked to him like an old friend, bringing up basketball, small talk from the office, the change in the weather.

Brett listened intently, nodding occasionally, as Lee helped him with the supper. "That was good," he remarked. "Better than hospital food. Do you know when they will let me out of here?" He stopped as if a thought had just occurred to him, "Where will I go when I get out?"

They looked at each other in surprise, "You have a home, Brett," Dave answered.

"I have a home? A house? Or...?"

"You have a house...and I...I'll come with you and take care of you...." She paused lest she reveal more than intended.

"Do I live alone?"

"Yes, you've been living alone."

"Tell me about myself."

Dave began, "You're a lawyer...the head of our law firm, Walker, Stevenson and Stevenson."

Thank you, Lord, she breathed, *thank you that he remembered not to call me Stevenson-Walker. I'm not sure he's ready to have a wife.*

"What kind of law do we practise?"

"We do a lot of corporate law...some family law...Leanne works in estates...." his voice trailed off as he noticed Brett attempting to analyse the information. "Actually, she's been working on her master's degree in Toronto; she hasn't been in the office in the last while."

"So...how old am I?"

"You're 32."

"How long have I been a lawyer?

"I'm not sure...probably about nine or ten years."

"Am I a good lawyer?"

"Very good!" they both nodded.

He smiled. "And I work with you two?"

More nods.

"Do we get along?"

"Very well!"

"Good!" He closed his eyes...pondering all he had learned...exhausted.

"Will you come tomorrow?" he asked as Dave prepared to go.

"You bet," he winked at Lee.

CHAPTER NINETEEN

"He's used to my constant attention. I'm not sure how he'll respond to my being gone for a week," she confided to Dave as they sat over coffee.

"Have you told him?"

"Yes. He says he'll be fine, but he looks stressed when we talk about it."

"He's walking pretty well...don't you think? Course he has those handrails on both sides to help him. I imagine that limp will evaporate as time goes on. Have they tried him on the walker yet?"

"I think today is the day. I'll be there, of course. He tries really hard...getting impatient to get out. I'm glad he wants to get better. Good thing this bail hearing will be over with before then. Don't know what we'd do if he was at home now," her jumbled thoughts spilled out as Dave listened in slight amusement. "So what are you grinning about?"

"You. You really love this guy, Lee. Don't know how you stayed away from him so long."

"I thought he stayed away from me. Guess that's why I'm afraid to tell him I'm his wife...what if...what if...?" Tears stung her eyes.

"Don't even go there, Sis," he took her hand across the table. "The guy is nuts about you...that's why he's in that bed...he ignored the storm because you said he could come."

"I know...I know...but what if he decides differently once he remembers?"

"We'll just leave all that in God's hands, sugar plum. He'll probably fall in love with you all over again!" She had to smile in spite of her tears.

"I wish I felt more prepared for this," she confided as they approached Toronto on the 401. "It's been a long time since I've really done any court work...feel quite unsure since my illness...and now Brett's."

"You'll do okay, honey bug. You're very fluent...you always look so confident, and you're convincing. The impact statements from the victims will be brought forward...my fear is that they might decide...since he's spent so much time in rehab that he can hit the streets again."

"I know...and I have to go back to class at least a few days every month...a week would be a lot better...keep me in touch...guess I can do my research in London and on the web, but...you know what I'm saying...any time I spend in Toronto I'd feel like a sitting duck."

"Either Bob or I will go with you, Lee. You wouldn't be going in there alone. When is your next exam?"

"Two weeks from tomorrow. And I hate to take either of you from the office. Bob's not even oriented yet."

"He's doing great, Lee. You know Bob...he's not going to leave any ground unturned. A better man we won't find. Sure hope Brett agrees to keeping him on...we need to pray that there won't be any tension when he gets back."

"Tension?"

"You know...about our having brought him in; Bob is especially nervous about that."

"Why is that? Brett will know we needed someone to help...however temporarily."

"I know, but he rather resents your relationship with Bob...sees him as an old boy friend... or whatever.

"I think you have a very vivid imagination. He and I discussed my friendship with Bob long before we ever dated. He knows better than that."

"I'm not sure...he's been really resistant to bringing him on board...he may feel ganged up on."

Dave eased into the crowded parking space and they hurried to find the right courtroom. "Looks like we're just on time," he said, noting the crowd overflowing into the hall. "Good thing we have reservations," he smirked, as they made their way to the prosecutor's bench.

"This will surely take all week," Leanne noted as she perused the documents. "17 to give testimony...68 impact statements. I hope they won't take time to read all of them in court."

"Whatever works, Lee...whatever works. We'll stay as long as we have to...just so justice is served and the public is safe."

The week had been long and brutal. Testimony of the witnesses had hung together. A few had been discredited...becoming flustered during cross examination. Defence Counsel had badgered mercilessly. Lee was not one to lose her composure. She gave her testimony as Dave expected...confidently...well organized...evidence in hand. Dave spoke on behalf of the group and argued brilliantly that Lonnie Hencken should be classified "a dangerous offender." He should never again be allowed to roam at will. He had proven himself not only a sexual predator, but had been caught red-handed at attempted murder.

Smiling and confident the elder Hencken had argued that while his son had been guilty of some misdemeanours, he nevertheless had undergone treatment and his chemical imbalance had been dealt with. The psychiatrist had corroborated his arguments with evidence, producing charts and notes which he entered as evidence of the change in psychological behaviour patterns. The elder lawyer noted the obvious...his client had already served two years of the ten-year sentence...albeit in a treatment facility...and his appeal would be forthcoming. He would pose no risk to society.

In the end, bail had been granted. Lonnie would wear a monitor for the first three months. He would stay clear of the university and other educational institutions...he would not be allowed to instruct or otherwise be involved with students...he would report twice weekly to a parole officer and keep his appointments at the psychiatric hospital. Then, taking into account the superficial confidence Defence Counsel displayed in his client's rehabilitation, and his own gut feeling, the experienced judge set bail at a half-million dollars.

"I know it isn't funny...what happened today," Leanne giggled, "but he sure made Hencken put his money where his mouth is."

"You got that right." Dave drove easily...his mood pensive. "Don't quite know about you going back to class...with him on the loose. Saw him glaring at you a time or two. Do you think he's...?" he stopped, not wanting to frighten her.

"I saw him, too. I don't think he'll be any different...just the sight of him is scary. He's lost a lot of weight...looks sick, don't you think? But...they have restricted him pretty good...I mean...the monitor...and he has to keep away from the university, and all."

"But he doesn't have to keep away from you. He knows where you live. He can watch to see if you are there...when you come and go. Lee, you must have a chaperone–a male chaperone–at all times when you're not in the classroom."

"You're giving me the shivers."

"Better a few shivers than strangling. I'll go with you. I'll take my lap top and work in the library while you're in class...stay with you at the condo at night. That way, if Brett comes out of his memory loss, he won't have to worry about Bob being with you."

"You know that Ian and Liz are still there...course they aren't always in the evening...."

"Ian? Oh, yeah, I forgot about him. Is he more than a tenant, Lee?"

"His wife would hardly approve. Why would you think that?"

"Don't know...maybe something Brett alluded to."

"That man! Why didn't he just ask? So you'll come with me? We'll have to be there a week from Monday...my exam is Tuesday at 8:00. Then I'll need a few days...."

CHAPTER TWENTY

"Pray with me that Brett will recognize home...that something will jog his memory. I wish he was well enough to take to Toronto. I'd sure like Dr. Hayes to see him. I wonder if he'd have any ideas...." She paused as Dave wheeled the minivan into the hospital parking area.

"We'd best leave him in God's hands, Sis. He knows when the time is right... though I confess my timing would be quite different," he smiled.

"And I have to confess that I'm scared out of my wits. He's so independent...in a helpless sort of way," she chuckled. "Whatever will I do if I can't handle him? He can be a bit stubborn."

"A bit? Come on now! But he's usually reasonable, and we'll only be a phone call away. With a nurse coming every day and home care...you won't be all alone."

He was in the wheelchair and ready to go, though Leanne noted that his smile couldn't hide the stress lines around his mouth...the fear in his eyes. *Poor man...wonder what he's thinking...what his fears are. Lord God, help me do all I can to make him feel he belongs...that he's valued...needed.*

"So is this where I live? Is this my house?"

Lee felt a keen sense of disappointment in his lack of recognition. She was so sure it would jog something in his memory. She nodded, "Yes, this is it? A very nice place...you'll be really comfortable...." she paused as he gripped the arm rest in the vehicle. Obviously he was more stressed than she realized. Another prayer followed as they stopped at the door and Dave unloaded the wheelchair.

"I'll just show you around a bit before you settle in...that way you'll be more at home...know your way around," Dave commented as he wheeled him slowly into the comfortable living room. "I think you call this the 'family room'," then continued into the dining room...the kitchen...the guest room that Brett had used for so many months. His bed had been replaced by the adjustable one that their father had used during his illness. They agreed he might find it easier to sit up by himself...get up to the bathroom. "The other bedroom is Leanne's," he said as he wheeled him back to the family room.

"Is something the matter?" Leanne asked uneasily.

"Yeah...I thought I might remember something...anything. Nothing registers."

So that's why he's so distressed...expecting too much of himself. Guess he must feel our anxiety for him to get well.

"It'll come...trying to rush won't help. Just take it easy," Dave encouraged.

"No kidding. We'll just take it one step at a time. Better rest and enjoy before we put you back in the harness," she attempted a smile. "Speaking of rest, you look all in. Would you like a nap before lunch?"

He nodded and Dave maneuvered the wheelchair through the bedroom door and it closed behind him.

Guess Dave will help him into bed...wonder if he'll let me help him next time. We can't have Dave running over here night and morning. I wonder if I should tell him he's my husband...if that would help...or hinder! Maybe I'll call Dr. Hayes.

"Join me for coffee before you rush off...a couple things I need to talk about."

Dave nodded and dropped into a chair at the kitchen table. "Do you think he'll let you help him dress? ...bathroom?"

"That's the first question. I can help him out of bed...to the bathroom door...he can stand alone...he should be okay once he has something to hold on to. He sure is reluctant to use the walker...maybe just a crutch for his weak side. Do you think that might work?"

He nodded, deep in thought. "Do you intend to serve all of his meals...do laundry... shopping...and still keep up with your school work?"

"I do. I did it before...of course I was working rather than in school. I can make meals ahead when I have time...and buy a few things ready-made. Today we'll have pizza...or at least he will...he's really fond of pepperoni-bacon. Hope his tastes are still the same," she shrugged.

"And your next question?"

"Well...next week when I go for my exam..." she paused, "I desperately need to spend a few days at the U. Any suggestions?"

"I've been thinking about that. Do you think...what about Uncle Ben and Aunt Maude? He could help Brett...she could do the cooking, etc."

"Do you think they might?"

"I think there's a really good chance. I'll stop by on my way home...let them think on it for a day or so. They've been asking if there's anything they can do," he grinned.

"They probably meant an errand or two...or maybe a casserole or fresh rolls...not the whole responsibility dropped in their lap."

"But they'd do well, don't you think?"

"No question about that."

CHAPTER TWENTY-ONE

She caught the phone on the second ring. "Mornin' missie, how's my little sis making out this morning?"

"We're both doing well, thank you, kind sir," she chirped.

"You sound like a spring robin...happily making her nest."

"Not quite...but I'm sure working toward that end. And what might occasion a mid-morning call from London's busiest lawyer?"

It was his turn to chuckle, "Not quite...but I'm sure working on it. Actually...I have Brett's brother here in my office and he would like to come and see him."

"Cut it, Dave...no funny stuff. You know Brett has no brother and my hands are pretty full with one Walker."

"Sorry...I thought you knew about his brother. Brett didn't tell you?"

"No way. He's an only child...an orphan."

"Well, almost! His mom died in childbirth and his brother was adopted by the doctor and his wife. He is now a doctor himself, Dr. James Wall...Brett just found out the week-end of the accident."

Her mind spun. "Maybe that's what he had to tell me...left a message on my answering machine...all excited about something...."

"Probably. James is most anxious to see Brett...he's called a few times and he's here now. Do you mind if he comes?"

"I'm not sure, Dave. Brett is plenty confused without throwing in a brother. I've told him he has no siblings...his parents gone. Does this man...James...know about Brett's memory problem?"

"Yes."

"Do you think it wise that he visit? Brett isn't big on doctors at

103

the moment...another new one...you get the picture?"

"Would you like to talk to him...explain your concerns?"

"Yes...that would be good."

"Hello, this is James Wall...and I am Brett's brother. I really would like to see him if you would allow me."

"Hello, Dr. Wall. You are quite the surprise...I take it you have met Brett?"

"Yes. I met him the day before the accident. Then I left for Toronto and Montreal for ten days, so I hadn't heard. I've been trying to see him but his office said he was recovering and wasn't allowed visitors."

"Well, I guess now you know why. He doesn't remember anyone. Doesn't remember who he is. He is very confused. I can imagine that you are anxious to see him...but I'd have to ask a couple of things of you."

"Certainly."

"I think it would be best if you don't tell him you're a doctor...he's had quite a lot of those lately."

"I can well understand that."

"And don't tell him you're his brother. I've just talked to his psychologist and he suggests we keep it simple...don't tell him anything he doesn't need to know right now. He's overwhelmed finding himself in a world that he can't remember, but in which he must somehow function. If we just let him find his way along...answer his questions...but not pressure him to remember. Do you understand what I'm trying to say?"

"Very much so. I'm happy to comply."

"We were just about to have morning coffee. Would you like to join us?"

The young man at the door was the picture of his older brother...sandy hair (windblown, she noted)...deep blue eyes...that determined chin...probably a little shorter than Brett, but just as handsome. They continued to appraise each other for a moment or two.

Leanne finally found her voice, "Well, there's no doubt about it...you're definitely his brother." She indicated the bedroom, "He'll be with us shortly."

"Thank you for letting me come. Can I ask who you are...are you his housekeeper? his nurse?"

"All of the above, I'm afraid. But I'm not a nurse, I'm a lawyer, and I'm his wife, Leanne Stevenson-Walker...." She stopped at the look on his face.

"I'm sorry...I didn't know he was married....he never...he didn't say anything when I met him that day in his office."

"I've been studying in Toronto...working on my master's degree."

"So...does he...did he remember you?"

"No. No, he didn't. He doesn't know he's married, so right now I'm just Leanne Stevenson...." She broke off as Brett slowly maneuvered himself through the door. He had finally given in to using the walker when the doctor refused to allow a crutch.

Leanne helped him to his chair, then noting the questioning look on his face, she offered, "Brett, this is James Wall. I invited him to have coffee with us."

"Hello, Brett. I was up to see you at the office the day before your accident. I wasn't expecting you to remember...just wanted you to know I care."

"That's good of you," Brett replied with a puzzled frown.

"Dave tells me you're doing really well...considering what you've been through."

"Guess I am...or so they tell me. I think I'm getting the hang of this walking business. I'll be glad to regain my memory...feel like I'm in a nether world...everybody knows everything but me."

"I can't imagine how that must feel. But you obviously remember quite a few things–how to eat...talk...."

Brett nodded slowly and Leanne rose to fill their cups. "I'll just leave you two for a few minutes," she said, as she headed to the computer desk in the family room. "Perhaps you can let me know when you're ready to leave, or when Brett needs help...whichever is first," she smiled.

"Did you enjoy visiting with James?" she asked as she straightened his bedding.

He nodded. "Yes, I did, he's really friendly...warm...attractive, I would say."

"Yes, he is attractive...but so are you, Brett Walker," she smiled, then paused as a worried look crossed his eyes.

"Is he your boyfriend?"

"No, Brett. I just met him this morning."

"Are you planning to leave me pretty soon?"

"Why would you think that?"

"I thought I heard you say something on the phone...about going to Toronto."

"Yes, I did say that. I've been going to university in Toronto and I have to go and write an exam and take some classes. I'll be gone about four days...but you don't need to worry, we have someone to come and stay with you. Do you remember meeting Uncle Ben and Aunt Maude?"

He nodded. "Are they my aunt and uncle?"

"No. They aren't ours either. Just really good friends."

"Are they my friends, too?"

"Yes. Very definitely. That's how I met you. Uncle Ben is a retired judge. He suggested you ask me to work for you when your secretary left. So you hired me, and I worked until I went back to finish my Law degree in Toronto. Now I'm working on a master's degree."

"Did you like working for me?"

"Yes, very much. Well...not at first...you were grouchy...but after we got to know each other, I enjoyed working for you."

"Did we like each other?"

"Oh, yes, we did. Now, I think you need to have a nap...we can talk again, if you like."

He smiled as she smoothed his hair and tucked the comforter around him.

The phone rang as she sat over her books. *That's Dave,* she smiled as she read the call display. "Hi, there."

"So how did that go?"

"All is quiet on the home front."

'James is really quite a guy, isn't he? A younger version of Brett. I look forward to getting to know him."

"No kidding! I'm impressed."

"So how did Brett respond to him?"

"They got on well...James kept the conversation going...led Brett from one topic to another. Never let on he was his kid brother. I'm going to make an appointment to see Paul Hayes when we're in town...you know...the psychologist. I'm really antsy about withholding information from Brett. He feels so out of it...if he at least knew.... I know where Paul is coming from...at least I think I do...he thinks we'd be adding pressure...making him feel even more responsibility to remember...."

"Have you thought of bringing him to the office, Lee? Or would that be more of the same?"

"I think I should ask him about that...after all he knows he's a lawyer and that he has an office. He may not feel ready for that. Maybe we could take him after hours when he wouldn't feel pressured to talk to a lot of folk he doesn't know."

"Good idea. Thought I'd stop by tonight after work for a few minutes...just so he doesn't forget who I am."

"No chance of that. He's sharp as a tack. What would you think about...?" she paused as she heard him moving in the bedroom. "Sorry, gotta' run."

She was surprised to find him sitting on the edge of the bed. "You're getting a bit too independent," she smiled as she came to help him to the bathroom.

"I could really do this by myself, you know, but then...."

"But then?"

"Then I'd miss having you put your arms around me," he smirked.

"You're a rascal, Brett Walker."

He stood looking at himself in the mirror, the words–*you're a rascal, Brett Walker*–ringing a bell in his brain. *You're a rascal, Brett Walker!* It turned over and over in his mind as she prepared him for the physiotherapist.

CHAPTER TWENTY-TWO

"Paul, I want you to meet my brother, Dave Stevenson. Dave...Dr. Paul Hayes."

"Glad you've come, Dave...good to see you again, Leanne. So...how's our boy doing?"

"We're not sure. We don't know what to expect. He's starting to ask questions about his past and I'm not sure how much to tell him."

"Does he understand what you tell him?"

"Oh, sure. And he remembers the names of people he meets...like Dave here...other acquaintances who drop by. Did he mention to you that he has a brother?"

He nodded. "He mentioned it to me the week-end of his accident. I suggested he not try to keep his appointment...guess he tried to come on the Saturday anyway. Not good! Not good at all!"

"Actually, it was my fault," Leanne's eyes watered, "he was coming to see me...said he had some exciting news to tell me...guess it must have been about his brother. He was over the other day...his brother, I mean...Dr. James Wall...a picture of Brett...super-nice!" She broke off at their smiles.

"Can you tell me again what happened between you and Brett that you let him come?"

She nodded. "I...I...guess it started with...with the pictures that our friend, Bob, took of our baby...and...and...Brett was holding her and weeping terribly...then he had her little white casket in his arms...." she couldn't go on.

"Take your time," he encouraged.

"I was just crushed. Thought Brett didn't care at all...either about

108

me or our baby...and then I saw him...so distraught...I...don't know what happened next. I think I started to pray...and knew that Brett and I should be together...to comfort each other...deal with our grief...and the phone rang...and it was Brett...and he wanted to come and I...wanted him to. Neither of us knew about the storm...."

"So he was coming to see you?"

She nodded through her tears.

Paul passed the box of tissues to Dave who was searching his pockets. "I guess we'd like some advice from you on how to handle things now," Dave suggested.

"Has he been to the office yet?" the doctor asked.

They both shook their heads. "He hasn't been terribly interested. He feels so out of it...everybody knows everything...about him and everything else...and he knows nothing. We were discussing taking him to the office after five and letting him get the feel of it. Right now our friend, Bob, is helping at the office...Brett doesn't realize what's going on. We don't know whether he'll approve once his memory returns...but we needed someone to help Dave."

"Good suggestions. He needs some stimulation without being put on the spot. I gather that he accepts Dave...and yourself...as his partners."

"He hasn't questioned that...or the fact that he heads up a law firm. He really likes Dave and looks forward to seeing him. He enjoyed visiting with James...though he doesn't know he's his brother...wondered if he was my boyfriend and felt a little threatened, I think."

"Good," the doctor smiled. "He has some emotions...he may feel that he has a claim on you and not know why...all that is good ...some residual memory kicking in."

"He heard us discussing coming to Toronto and was afraid I was planning to leave him, so I assured him that would not happen...just a few days to write an exam and catch up on some class work. He nodded as though he understood."

"How does he look now? Could he recognize himself...say on a photograph...or...?"

"I don't think so...his hair is beginning to look more normal...and his bruises are mostly gone...but he's growing a beard, and...he's lost a lot of weight. He looks quite a bit older than he did," she looked at Dave and he nodded in agreement.

"Can he be persuaded to part with the beard?"

"Possibly. I think he couldn't shave himself and had a hard time letting anyone else...so he just let it grow. I'll ask him. I guess...I'm wondering...what if he asks if I'm married...or if he's married? I feel like I'm deceiving him by not telling him I'm his wife...and that James is his brother."

"Not really. You don't deceive a child by not giving him all the details of how he got here. You tell him when the time is right...and I think you'll know when to tell Brett."

"Well...if we take him to the office...it may help things along."

"Does he show any signs of affection toward you...physically or otherwise?"

"Oh, sure. He's very complimentary...I catch him watching me. Likes me to help him out of bed...because I put my arms around him, he says. I'm wondering if I should be more... more...?"

Both men chuckled, causing her to blush.

"Being a little 'more...more' won't hurt a thing. He'll probably fall in love with you all over again!"

"Don't know if I can handle having two Bretts in love with me...the old one who knows all about me...and the new one...who doesn't know me at all."

"How do you think he might respond to Leanne if he finds out she's his wife? Can you give us a 'for instance'?" Dave asked.

"The better the relationship between them now, the better he'll respond, I would imagine. Later, if he—or when he—regains the memory loss, he'll congratulate himself for having the good sense to win her twice." They all chuckled.

"Well, let's just hope you're right," Leanne made no effort to conceal her skepticism.

"So what do you think stands in the way of regaining his memory?" Dave asked.

"It's hard to say. Could be a number of things...possibly a little residual swelling. Don't forget that he's good at blocking out unpleasant memories...some of it may be psychological; he's had a lot of pain."

Some of it may be psychological...some of it may be psychological. It echoed in Leanne's mind as they joined the many lanes of traffic heading toward London.

"You're awfully quiet. Great chat with Dr. Paul...don't you think?" her brother asked at length.

"I hope he knows what he's talking about with Brett. Really...I'm afraid to tell him and afraid not to. The possibility of a psychological block really frightens me...more of the same. I'm afraid of losing him all together. Guess I'd best commit him to the Lord...again!"

"You don't have to sweat that one. I was with him the night you left...he was beside himself...he was totally numb. For the life of me...I don't know how he got through that court case...the Lord just undertook for him. I wonder how Ben and Maude made out with him."

" They were doing well when I called yesterday. Aunt Maude asked about our time at the university and my exam...and whether we had seen any signs of Lonnie. I assured her all was well...no signs of Lonnie."

"Forget it, Lee...you can just forget it!"

"Forget what?" she feigned innocence.

"I know you too well...I know what you're thinking...and I want to assure you right now that you are not going to Toronto by yourself next time! Just because we didn't see Lonnie doesn't mean he isn't there...he'll be after you once he knows you're about. I repeat...you are not...not going alone.

CHAPTER TWENTY-THREE

"Do I get one of those, too?"

She turned from hugging Aunt Maude, to see Brett slowly approaching with only a cane for support.

"Brett," she squealed, as she moved toward him. "What are you doing without your walker?"

"I *am a Walker*," he joked. "Why would I need one? Besides, doc says my leg's almost good as new," he indicated only a bandage where the cast had been.

"I take my eyes off him for a few days and...."

His strong embrace caught her off guard. It felt so good to be in his arms. "I've missed you," he whispered.

"Missed you, too."

"We'll just get on home," Aunt Maude reached for her coat, "you'll find your supper in the warming oven, dear."

More hugs and kisses and thank-you's and Leanne sat down to a delicious plate of chicken stir-fry.

"I'm so glad you're home, Lee. I've missed you terribly."

She smiled warmly, noting that he had called her *Lee*. "I've missed you, too, Brett Walker. What did you do while I was gone? Did you and Uncle Ben enjoy each other?"

"Indeed, we did! He's quite a guy. Guess he's been helping Dave with some of my files and he brought them home to work on. I enjoyed going over some of the cases with him. I'm surprised at how much I remember."

"That's wonderful!" she exclaimed, and he noticed the twinkle in her eyes.

"And I've spent some time on the computer."

"Great news. You'll be back in the swing of things in no time."

"I asked Ben about...about us...." he hesitated at the look of concern on Lee's face.

"What did you want to know, Brett?"

"I'm not sure...just wanted to know...."

She waited. When he did not continue, she prompted, "to know...?"

"I don't know, Lee. Sometimes I feel like I should know you...some things are so familiar...and yet...."

"And yet...?"

"I don't know...I just can't get a handle on how things were between us. Can we talk about it some time?"

"Yes, we will, Brett. But I'm just too tired tonight, and tomorrow you have a doctor's appointment."

"Another one? With who?"

"The urologist." He nodded as she continued, "Maybe we could go to lunch. Would you like that?"

"I'm not sure–where would we go?"

"How about The Golden Dragon? It was one of our favourite Chinese...." she paused, realizing she had revealed more about their relationship than she intended.

"Did we go there often?"

"Sometimes after work. It's not a large place but the food is delicious. We could go around one o'clock...that way you probably won't meet anyone who knows you."

"Good, let's do it." Then pausing, he asked, "Do I have any money?"

"Of course you do...you're a lawyer after all," she chuckled.

"So where can I get some?"

"There is some in your wallet. They returned it with your briefcase after the accident. Or, we could go to the bank and get some. Do you know your number for the ATM?"

"ATM?"

"The automated teller machine...you know...where you put in your card and...?"

"Yes, I remember. But I don't think I know the number."

"It won't matter...they'll give you a new one, but you don't need money today...."

"Of course I do. I want to treat you to lunch. Will you bring my wallet?"

"Will you eat more than eighty dollars worth?" he grinned as he finished counting.

"I might if you're paying," she countered.

They exchanged a warm smile before he struggled to his feet. She slipped an arm around him and helped him to the sofa in the family room.

"Will you sit with me while we watch the news?" he asked, indicating the seat beside him.

She nodded and removed the morning paper before seating herself. "Are you warm enough?" she asked. "Would you like a blanket?"

"No...just you to sit with me. Do you mind?"

"Of course not. I enjoy sitting with you."

"Do you like me, Leanne?"

"Yes...very much."

"Do you have a boyfriend?"

"No, but I don't want to talk tonight."

"Are you afraid of something, Leanne?"

"Yes. I would have to say that I am."

"Can I ask why...why you're afraid?"

She chuckled. "You can ask all you want, but tonight you aren't getting any answers. I'm just too tired. We will talk, Brett. I'm not sure I can answer what you want to know, but we will give it our best shot. I'm going to get horizontal. Can I help you to bed before I do?"

"Thank you, Lee," he took her arm and let her help him up, forgetting that he intended to watch the evening news.

"See you in the morning," she smiled as she tucked him in.

His eyes sought hers for a long moment, then he gently pulled her to him and kissed her cheek. "You are so very lovely," he said softly.

CHAPTER TWENTY-FOUR

"I'll back the car out; it will be easier for you to get in," she suggested as she headed to the garage. "Just wait until I come in, and I'll help you."

His happy smile vanished as they stepped out onto the driveway. "No," he stated emphatically. "No, I'm not going in that...that...*purple thing!*"

"Whatever...whatever is the matter with you, Brett Walker? Is there something wrong with my car? You've ridden in it before!"

"I have not! And I'm not going to!"

"Whatever is the matter?" she repeated.

"I'm sorry. I didn't mean to shout at you. I can't. I just can't. It's...I'm not sure. It's *purple!*" He faltered. "Is it yours?"

"Of course it's mine! Come, We'll get you back in the house. Maybe Dave can help us out," she suggested as she called her brother.

Ten minutes later Dave pulled away with the *purple thing* and Brett happily enjoyed the passenger seat in the minivan.

Leanne turned her face to hide her smirk. *You do keep life interesting, Brett Walker!*

"Well, you certainly got a good report from the doctor," she commented as they sat over lunch at The Golden Dragon. "Are you enjoying the food? Did I remember correctly?"

He nodded. "You know me pretty well, don't you?" His eyes searched her face.

"Yes." Hastening to change the subject she asked, "Would this be a good day to visit the office...after you've had your nap, I mean?"

Noting his discomfort, she added, "We'll go around five...just the lawyers and staff will be there."

"Will Ben Davis be there?"

"I'm not sure, but I'll call and see. Would you like him to be?"

"Yeah, I'd like that."

She called the office on her cell, then explained, "It looks like Ben has another commitment today. They suggest tomorrow. Okay?"

He nodded.

"Would you like to go for a little tour around the town...maybe go by our office building? We could take a short walk in Spring Bank Park first if you like, since we're so close here," she looked at him questioningly.

He nodded. "Maybe I'll remember something."

They walked slowly, savouring the quiet, enjoying the crisp atmosphere, the sun filtering through the leafless beech and oak. A squirrel scolded, then scampered higher and disappeared among the bare branches.

"Did we come here often?"

His question caught her off guard. "Yes, it's a very popular spot...especially in the summer," she managed.

"Did you and I come here?"

"Sometimes."

"Just the two of us?"

"Sometimes." Then as an afterthought, she suggested, "Well, perhaps we'd better get on with our little tour."

She's done it again...avoided my question. What is it that she can't talk about? he pondered as they drove.

"That's it...the office building, isn't it?"

She smiled. "Right you are. Do you want to go up, or shall we leave it for tomorrow?"

"Well, if we leave it for tomorrow...then maybe we can have our visit this afternoon?" He looked at her for approval.

"Sure, we can do that. How about right after your nap?"

"I'm too excited to nap."

"Why is that?"

"Because I have too many things going on in my head."

"Well, then, I better get you home and relieve the pressure before we have a blowout in that brain of yours."

His look of smug satisfaction amused her, as she headed back around the block. *You really are a rascal, Brett Walker!*

"Why are you stopping here? I don't want to go to McDonald's."

"You don't have to. I'll just be a minute."

"No. Don't go in there. No."

"Cut it, Brett. I have to have a bathroom stop. Can I get you a coffee?"

"No. Not here!"

"Brett. I need a bathroom. I'll be right out." *Whatever can be the matter with that man? His face...he's absolutely paranoid.*

"Now then," she began, presenting him with a coffee, "tell me why you are having a jolly fit about my stopping at McDonald's."

"I'm not sure," he stammered as he struggled to conquer the fear showing on his face.

"So...maybe we should start with those things that are going on in your head," she suggested as she turned up the thermostat in the family room. "Tell me what you're thinking."

"I'm thinking..." he paused, then winked at her before he continued, "...we must have known each other quite well." His eyes questioned her.

"Yes. I think I've already mentioned that. But why do *you* think so?"

"Because you know your way around my house...and around me. You know how I like to have my back and shoulders rubbed...where my clothes are...what I like to eat...."

"I'd forgotten some things about you, Brett...like how sharp you are!"

He smiled and waited for her to comment further. "So what else are you thinking?"

"That I'd like to know more about us...about you. I'd like to know what kind of a relationship we had...were we special friends? lovers?"

he finished

"What would you like to know about me, Brett?"

"I'd like to know if you have someone special in your life now? and if it's James Wall."

"No, James Wall is not a special friend. I'm sure I've mentioned a time or two that I only met James when he came here to see you. I had never seen him before that."

"And the rest of the question?"

He really doesn't miss a thing. Oh, God, help me. Shall I tell him he's the special man in my life...my husband?

He watched her struggle. "Have I put you on the spot? Is there something you don't want me to know?"

"Yes...you've got me on the witness stand. I don't want to hide anything from you, Brett. I...I wish...I mean, I would have liked you to remember me in your own time...Dr. Hayes felt it would be best if you just...I mean if you were able to...."

"Just tell me, Lee."

"Yes," she whispered, "there is a special man in my life."

"James Wall?"

"No! Why do you keep asking?"

"He keeps coming."

"He comes to see you...he...." she closed her eyes and prayed again. *Oh, God, help!*

"So...can I ask about this special...?"

She nodded. "You're special to me, Brett."

"How special?"

She sat on the edge of his chair and ran her fingers through his hair. "Very, very special!"

He pulled her gently onto his lap and held her to him. She could feel his heart speeding up and wondered what effect it might have on the lung that had been punctured. It felt so good to be in his arms...and to snuggle into his neck.

His kisses moved down her forehead...her nose...her lips as they responded to his. "I love you, Lee...I love you," he repeated between kisses. "Do you care that much for me?"

She nodded. "Yes, I love you, too, "she whispered, and held out her hand. "Come," she stood and helped him up. They paused inside the master bedroom, and she indicated the beautifully framed portrait of the radiant bride looking into her husband's eyes.

She felt him stiffen. "So you're married? ...to James Wall?" his voice wavered in anguish.

"No...no! That isn't James Wall."

"Don't do this to me, Leanne....of course it is. Why did you tell...?"

"Maybe you should shave off that beard and take another look in the mirror," she suggested.

"Are you saying that's me?" He moved closer and took a long look at the man in the portrait...then turned to look at himself.

"So...I'm married? *To you?* " he yelled, "and you didn't tell me?"

He stood immobilized, hearing the garage door open and close, the vehicle fading in the distance. He tried to focus on the radiant bride, but his mind saw only the anguish–the face drained of colour...the sadness in the beautiful grey-green eyes–as she turned and slipped from the room.

The angry face of the man in the mirror struck a nerve. There was something too familiar about this scenario.... He picked up the ring box on the dresser and ran his fingers over the jewelled lid...inside the expensive diamonds sparkled up at him...too, too familiar....

"O God, help!" He stopped to ponder what he had just done. He had called on God! Why had he done so? It had come so naturally, as though...as though...as though God were reaching out to him. Well...he'd just try it again. "Please, God, help me to know what to do...with myself...with Leanne. I seem to have made these mistakes before...they're so familiar. You're familiar, too, God...Please, help me to remember the things that always elude me but seem to echo in my mind."

"Please ask Dr. Hayes to call me when he has time." She closed her cell phone and sat back to contemplate. *I should have asked him to call on my cell,* she berated herself. *Oh, well, I'll be home by the*

119

time he calls. She sipped her coffee slowly between prayers...thoughts... plans, as she watched the snow flakes slowly melting on the windshield of the van.

O Lord, God. You know about Brett.... She paused as tears overwhelmed her. *You know I was afraid to tell him we were married...afraid he'd be angry and reject me...and I was afraid not to tell him...because...because....* She pulled a tissue from the box and blew her nose...*because he'd be angry. Now I've done both and he is angry–very angry.... I guess I feel...I have always felt–since my pregnancy at least–that he really doesn't want me...doesn't want a wife. But Lord, my promise still stands...I'll stay and care for him like I promised. Just show me how, Lord...I so desperately want to do your will.*

He stumbled in his attempt to hurry before it quit ringing. It might be Leanne.

"Is Leanne there, please?" he noted the professional voice.

"No, I'm sorry, she just stepped out."

"This sounds like Brett. Do you remember me? I'm Dr. Paul Hayes."

"Yes...well...no...not really, but Leanne speaks of you. She would like me to see you when we are next in Toronto."

"I'll look forward to that. Is that why she was calling today?"

" I...don't think so. I'm not sure...I...I guess I have a lot of questions that she doesn't want to answer and today...well...she told me we're married."

"And?"

"And I was so shocked...I yelled at her."

"And?"

"And she left–just got in the van and drove away."

After a lengthy silence, Paul asked, "How long ago, Brett?"

"I don't know–maybe an hour–seems like forever."

"I'm sure it does. So tell me how you feel about Leanne–how you feel about being married to her."

"I wish I would have known from the beginning; it would have made things so much easier. Are there other monumental secrets that are going to change my life?" Paul noticed the edge to his voice.

"Yes, I would have to say there are. And I need to tell you that it was not Leanne's choice to withhold the marriage information...it was mine. I felt it might be too much responsibility to lay on you at one time...especially since the relationship had broken down...."

The gasp on the other end of the phone stopped the flow of information.

"I'm sorry; I didn't realize you didn't know."

"Is someone going to tell me about this? Are you?"

"Brett, do you still have the tapes of our counselling sessions?"

"I'm not sure what you're talking about."

"The last three or four sessions you had with me...and some I had with Leanne...we recorded them and you each have a copy. I suggest you listen to them, and many of your questions will be answered. I seriously doubt that Leanne will volunteer further information after what you've just described. She was fearful...seems she knows you quite well."

"Well, maybe I'd best get to it, then."

CHAPTER TWENTY-FIVE

She paused at the door to the family room; the voice was definitely Brett's...he must have company. The scene on the television screen immobilized her...fascinated her. She had not watched the wedding video since shortly after their honeymoon...the tiny flower girl in her purple frilly gown with her basket of petals...the ring bearer in his white tuxedo proudly holding the lacy cushion with the ring...the bride.... *My wedding day!...how happy and excited I am!* The camera focused on Brett. *What a gorgeous man!...looking at me with such devotion! Whatever happened to us, Lord?*

He sensed her presence and turned...wiping his face on his sleeve in an attempt to hide the tears. He touched the *pause* button as she moved to sit beside him.

"I...I found this in the cabinet," he indicated the entertainment centre. "Dr. Hayes suggested I listen to the tapes...the ones we recorded of our sessions with him...and I was looking for them when I found this."

She nodded. *He's very upset...acting like he's been caught with his hand in the cookie jar. Where do we go from here?* Trying to keep her voice even, she suggested, "Why don't we finish watching it?"

He continued his vows, "...for better–for worse...for richer–for poorer...in sickness and in health...until death...."

She covered her face with her hands and let the tears come. Awkwardly he placed an arm around her, then wiped his tears on his sleeve, before he again touched the *pause* button.

"I'm sorry, Lee, so very sorry," he sobbed brokenly. "What happened to us? What did I do to cause the breakdown of...of...?

Can you...will you tell me?"

"I don't know what...or why it happened," she sobbed. "You wanted a child...and when I got pregnant...."

"A child? We have a child?"

"No, no we don't have a child, Brett."

"But you were pregnant; did you miscarry? abort?"

"None of the above. Our baby died shortly after birth."

"Why?" he asked brokenly.

"Because I had been sick and they couldn't find the problem. Then they found Celiac Disease a month before she was born...she was a month premature...."

"So the Celiac Disease caused...?"

She nodded. "It's an allergy to gluten found in wheat and other grains. It disables the small intestine so the food isn't digested. Both of us suffered from malnutrition...she had breathing problems, possible brain damage...."

"So it was a little girl?"

"Yes."

"Can you tell me...how old...how long she lived?"

"I think only a few hours while they worked on her. I never saw her; I was unconscious, but you were there, and Dave and...others."

"Do we have any pictures of her?"

She nodded. "Bob Wilson took pictures and sent them to me on CD."

"So...what happened? Did this...." he paused, not knowing how to ask, "Did this... " he began again, "...cause trouble? Dr. Hayes said that we...that our relationship...?"

"I don't think I can answer that, Brett; maybe you'd better listen to the tapes."

"It's so bad you can't talk about it?"

"I don't know what happened. You just withdrew from me once I got pregnant...you didn't want me any more," she was crying again, trying to stifle the tears...the lump in her throat.

"No...no...that can't be true. I love you, Leanne. I know I loved you before...."

"If I believed that..." she paused to get control of her emotions. "I need to get supper started," she added, "why don't you finish the video? I'll call when it's ready."

"Please don't go. I need you to help me...help me remember." He reached for her hand. Please, Leanne, please."

She allowed him to pull her back beside him.

"I know I must have hurt you terribly...I don't know why...or how...but I ask your forgiveness. Will you forgive me...help me to understand?"

"I'm not harbouring a grudge, Brett. I'm not trying to get even."

"Dr. Hayes said something about you being afraid of me." When she didn't respond, he continued, "Are you afraid of me?"

"No. And yes."

"Will you explain that?"

"When I first went to work for you, Brett, you were a very angry man; you raised your voice whenever you disliked or disagreed with anyone, or anything. I got in the habit of just leaving in order to avoid confrontation. You stopped doing that before we were married, then started again when I was pregnant...before you left me"

"Are you afraid of me now?"

"Yes." He motioned for her to continue. "I love you, Brett. I have never stopped loving you...I tried though. You think you love me now, but when your memory returns...will you realize why you left me...and do it over again? Am I afraid? Of course, I am. You'll do it over again...." He watched her lovely eyes fill with tears.

"No...I won't, Leanne. I promise you I won't."

He sat quietly for so long she wondered where his thoughts had taken him. When at last he spoke, he took her by surprise, "Will you listen to the tapes with me, Lee, so we can talk about these things?"

"I don't know...give me time to think it over. It might be best if you discussed the tapes with Dr. Hayes...he had been helping you work through some of your bad dreams.... Why don't you finish the wedding," she motioned to the television, "while I start supper?"

He sat thinking of what he had seen so far...obviously the wedding was as beautiful as the ceremony was sacred. The bridesmaids were gowned in varius shades of mauve and purple... groomsmen in black. *That must have been my choice...white tux for me...black for the groomsmen.* Dave had escorted Lee down the aisle...*what a vision of loveliness she was...*and given her to him. *We were so in love...we still are...she loves me...she said so...and I know I love her...will love her always. I need to find out what happened to us...to me...to make me do that to her. God help me!*

She let the phone ring until he picked it up. "It's Dave," he called. "They would like us to have supper with them after we go to the office tomorrow."

"It's okay with me."

"Sure, we'd be glad to come," she heard him continue chatting with Dave, and thanked the Lord that some things seemed to be almost normal.

CHAPTER TWENTY-SIX

His words caught her by surprise as she refilled his coffee, "Can we read the Bible and pray together this morning?"

"Love to," she smiled.

"And I think I need to work on finances today...find out how things are with us...what we're living on and...."

"And what, Brett?"

"I don't know what I don't know, Lee. Will you help me...go over things with me...tell me where to look to find out what I need to know? I'd like to get my hair cut first."

"Sure. We could go to the bank...after the haircut. Maybe we should do that this morning so you can get your personal accounts in order. That might be all you can handle in one day. And, if you're feeling up to it, we can go over the business...."

"Maybe Dave will fill me in on the office accounts."

"Good idea. I really think you'll be quite weary by the time we go to the bank, then the office in late afternoon, and Dave and Sherry's for supper."

"I'll just get my Bible," he said as he headed to his room. "I found it in my briefcase yesterday when I was looking for the tapes from Dr. Hayes."

"Did you find the tapes?"

"I'm not sure how many there were. I found three. I may have had some on the seat in the car...could have lost some in the accident."

Their conversation delighted her–he was sounding a little more normal every day–wanting financial responsibility, showing some spiritual leadership. *Thank you, God, for every positive change.*

"I guess I must've been reading through the Psalms...my marker is at Psalm 85. Okay if I read it?"

"Please do."

He proceeded to read the prayer of David, then paused, "I noticed last night when I was reading that I had highlighted verse 11. It's really special." He proceeded:

Teach me your way, O Lord, and I will walk in your truth;
give me an undivided heart, that I may fear your name.

And then it says:

I will praise you, O Lord my God, with all my heart;
I will glorify your name forever.
For great is your love toward me;
You have delivered me from the depths of the grave.

"That's a powerful passage Brett; .Tell me how it speaks to you."

"I wish I knew what it meant to me at the time I marked it. I must have been seeking the Lord's direction to walk in his truth...praying my heart wouldn't be divided."

O Lord, God...what a lesson for me...an undivided heart...undivided indeed!

"And then the part about delivering me from the grave," he went on, "he certainly did that for me and I want to praise and thank him.... How come we don't go to church any more?"

She chuckled as she followed his train of thought. *A logical conclusion...we need to praise and thank God in the assembly of believers....*

"I didn't think you were ready for that many people at once...especially since you wouldn't remember too many. Would you like to go this coming Sunday?"

"I think I should at least give it a try...I'll be okay if you stay with me."

"Yes, I'll do that, and Dave and Sherry will be there, too, and others you know. Would you like to pray before we head out, or shall I?"

"Why don't you pray today, and I will tomorrow."

"How shall I pray for you?"

"Pray I'll understand...remember what's important at the bank...the office."

She smiled as he reached for her hand. *Like old times,* she decided.

She watched him adjust his tie in front of the mirror. *With that hair cut and beard gone, he's his handsome self...the guy I fell for!*.

"Am I okay?" She noted his obvious nervousness.

"Better than okay. Just as handsome as the man in my bedroom."

He grinned. "Are you going to let this man back in there one of these days, too, or...?"

"Or?"

"Or is the man on the wall all you want?"

O God...it's me again! Help! "You're moving too fast for me, Brett. Let's take it one day at a time. I would really like you to remember...."

"Come on now; I haven't forgotten *everything*!" he smirked.

"You are an absolute rascal, Brett Walker!"

"Unco Bwett," the tiny blonde, blue-eyed cherub hurled herself at him. Without a second thought, Brett caught her in his arms and whirled her around, as she squealed in delight.

"Looks like you've done that a time or two," Lee remarked.

"She's been asking for you," Sherry explained, "and I told her you were coming for supper. Poor Unco Bwett will get to read the entire toddler shelf."

He smiled as she made herself at home in his lap and opened her favourite *Dr. Seuss.*

"Weed me," she pointed her chubby fingers at the cat with the hat.

Leanne watched fascinated as he read the same thing over and over. *What a wonderful father he would be. No wonder he wanted a child so badly...hmmm!*

"So how did you feel your time at the office went?" Dave asked as they enjoyed an after-dinner Cappuccino.

"Better than expected. I was pretty rattled, until I realized that I knew both Becky and Melva, and could find my way around. I felt at home in my office. Where have you put Bob? I didn't see him."

"He had to leave early. He used your office, unless Uncle Ben came in. Then, he worked in the library. It was really awkward for everybody–especially him–but we needed his help and he was willing to come even though I couldn't offer him long-term."

"What does he bring to the office that we need?"

"Good question," Dave smiled. *This sounds like the Brett I know.* "Bob took extra studies in Corporate Law...he's really interested in that area; it was something I had to learn on the job; I took only the preliminaries. Besides that, I know him really well, we grew up together, have worked together at times. I guess you know that we lived together at University. He's steady, thorough, doesn't leave any ground unturned to get to the facts."

"Sounds like somebody we should take on board long term. Is he interested?"

"You bet!"

"Good. Let's get together with him in a week or so and see what we can come up with. I'd like to start coming in for a while every day...maybe mornings would be best. Sorry I've taken so long to come to this point."

"No fault of yours. Are you sure you're up to all that much?"

"Won't know till we try. I'll have to depend on Leanne to drive me until I can get wheels and medical clearance."

"You know I'm happy to drive, but the wheels *are* purple." Noting his stress, she added, "We can't keep Dave's van indefinitely."

"Maybe I'll have to rent something until I have wheels," he feigned a smile.

We absolutely must get to the bottom of this 'purple' business. "So where will we put Bob?" she changed the subject.

"I've been wondering about the little room next to my office," Dave looked at Brett.

"Awfully small."

"But the window is a good size; if we could get the storage room next to it...knock out the wall...viola!"

"You may be right. Have you discussed this with Bob?"

"We've looked at possibilities...of course we didn't know if you'd approve of taking on another partner...and we were way too busy to put any effort into it."

"You've been awfully quiet, Lee. What do you think of taking on another partner? Obviously you know Bob. What about him? Do you agree with Dave?"

"No question we need another partner...we're behind in some very important corporate matters. Losing the confidence of clients is not something we can afford. On the other hand, we will have to do a careful review of our finances–now and down the road. Bob will need a salary...and we'll need another secretary...at least part time."

"Very well put, my love. What about Bob?"

"We won't do better. Do you remember him?"

"Don't remember a whole lot. What I do is positive. Let's take a week then, and look over our situation...and the possibilities."

He was still whistling happily as she parked in the garage. "Take it easy, there, I'll give you a hand," she suggested as he attempted to exit the van."

"I'm practising...need to be less dependent...on you...and everybody."

What he leaves out always speaks volumes. "I know you're anxious to be independent, but we'd all like you to get there safely," she took his arm and handed him his cane. "So...let's just take it cool...you've come a long way...."

He removed his arm from her grasp and slipped it around her waist as they made their way into the house.

"You've had quite a day," she suggested as they sat over hot cider in the family room. "How do you feel about...?"

"Like I'm beginning to come alive...maybe a little more human," he smiled.

"Tell me something, Brett. I am curious–make that extremely curious–why you have such a problem with my Lexus. Is it just the colour? or?"

"It's the whole thing!"

"Do you know why?"

"I'm not sure. Is it yours?"

"Of course."

"How did you get it? Did someone give it to you?"

"I bought it."

"With what?"

"Money!"

"Where did you get that much money?"

"It was a gift."

"And that was okay with you? ...you just accepted ...?"

"What is it that's troubling you, Brett. Of course I just accepted it. Why wouldn't I?"

He contemplated what she had just said. "Why would you?"

"Because it was an annuity from my father; it matured, and I used a portion of it to buy the car. I paid cash...." she stopped, noting the relief on his face. "Where did you think I got it? Who did you think gave it to me?"

"I didn't remember what upset me so much...guess I thought...I thought maybe...."

"Maybe?"

"I'm not sure right now."

"But I have clearance to drive the Lexus? ...or do I have to change the colour?"

"No. I don't mind the colour and I think you really like it."

"Mom and I were both wild about purple...and I guess I ordered it...well, it reminds me of her...guess I thought she'd be pleased to see me–if she sees me–driving it...." she turned away to hide the tears that suddenly stung her eyes.

"Leanne," he said softly, taking her hand. "I am so sorry for all the pain I've caused you since we married...and before. I'm going to listen to all of our sessions with Dr. Hayes, and then I want to try and be the husband you deserve...the one God wants me to be. Guess I can start by accepting your offer to chauffeur me in the purple chariot."

She smiled and planted a warm kiss on his cheek, "Thank you, Brett Walker."

CHAPTER TWENTY-SEVEN

"Do you want to go out for lunch today, since we'll be at the office? or shall I take something? or maybe you'd like to come home...? Guess we'll be home around one, won't we?"

"Any of the above, or maybe we could have some sandwiches brought up like we used to," he grinned, obviously proud of himself for remembering.

"Pretty sharp, there, Brett Walker! But I can't have bread, remember?"

"Have you always called me *Brett Walker?* or...?" she noticed him blush.

"Sometimes I called you other things," she teased.

"Are you going to enlighten me?"

"Guess I haven't had a pet name for you like you do for me, but I have called you *my love* or *my beloved;* I often called you *dearest, sweetheart,* sometimes *darling.* "

"How come you don't any more?"

"I'm not sure...guess I got out of the habit of having a husband."

"Will you get back in the habit any time soon?"

"Of course, my love," she smiled as she cleared the breakfast table.

"Do you remember that young doctor that came to visit us a couple of times?" he asked as they drove toward the office building.

"Yes, of course...Dr. James Wall."

"Can you tell me about him? Is he a client...or a friend...or...? Nothing comes up on my mental screen?"

"Oh dear! Oh dear! Oh dear!"

"That bad, huh?"

"Not bad...not bad at all.... What's bad is that I had intended to tell you about him some time ago, and then lost it from *my* mental screen." She chanced a quick look at him as she maneuvered through the morning traffic. "Tell me, Brett," she continued, "tell me what you remember about your family. Do you remember your home, your mom and dad?"

"Yes, I remember quite a bit about my childhood."

"And do you remember that you were an only child?"

"Yes."

"Well...sorry...I don't know how to say this...but you learned just before your accident that you have a younger brother–James Wall."

He sat in stunned silence watching the wipers as they slapped the gathering snowflakes back and forth across the windshield. She glanced at him several times before he finally spoke.

"And how did I learn about this brother?"

"He called on you at the office and introduced himself. You were both thrilled to discover you had a brother. You called me the next day and mentioned that you had a wonderful surprise and asked if you could come and see me? I said you could...only I didn't know about the ice storm."

He leaned back and closed his eyes...trying desperately to recall.

"So I must have believed he's my brother?"

"Yes, definitely. You told Dave all about it. Your mom was very ill before James was born...she knew she was dying, and your father had just learned that he had Lou Gehrig's Disease, so they adopted him out to Dr. & Mrs. Wall. Since the Walls couldn't have children of their own, they were delighted–still are."

"He certainly looks like me."

"Yes...yes he does. He's a lot like you, too, Brett...wears his hair the same...dresses quite a bit like you do...has a delightful smile...warm...friendly. I think he's a little shorter than you...probably around the six-foot mark, I would say."

"You like him, don't you?"

She nodded. "That didn't take any effort–a carbon copy of his big brother!"

"You're a special lady, Mrs. Walker."

She returned his smile before she swung into the parkade.

CHAPTER TWENTY-EIGHT

She could hear the discussion with Dr. Hayes as she slipped out of her coat and boots. Brett seemed to be responding to one of her sessions with the psychologist. He sat with his head in his hands as the taped conversation progressed.

Sensing her presence in the doorway, he looked up, his face drenched with tears. His finger touched the remote and the voices ceased. Again he buried his face in his hands and gave way to great wrenching sobs.

"Sweetheart," she slipped down beside him and put her arms around his heaving shoulders. "What can be so terrible?" she asked, reaching for the tissue box.

"Oh, Lee, I am so sorry!"

"What...?" she stumbled, not knowing where to begin. "Can you talk about...about what is causing you so much pain?"

"I'm remembering...when I hear you telling about our marriage...and...and your illness...I remember it happening...." he continued wiping at the stubborn tears, "and I don't know what happened to our happiness."

"Dr. Hayes thinks it's something to do with your past. He thinks you had a dream that was so terrible you blocked it out, you know...like you did with the abuse you went through in the group home. Do you remember that...or was it on one of the tapes?"

"I remember the abuse, the nightmares, and discussing it with him, but that was before we married."

"I know, dearest, but Dr. Hayes did think it significant that you numbed out when I was pregnant and sick; he thinks there might be an emotional link between your mom's illness when she was pregnant...." her voice trailed off at the look on his face.

"I'm sure he's right. Now that I think on it, I felt the same fear...she looked all white and shaky...she lost the babies–at least two or three, I think–and then she died."

"Guess I should ask how you responded to her when she was pregnant...when she got so sick."

"I must have just numbed it out. Paul thinks I'm really practised at numbing; that's the way I was when we met, if you remember."

She nodded. "Tell me what numbing-out feels like."

"It doesn't feel like anything. Emotions are blocked out. He explained that we all use mechanisms...or techniques, or whatever, to help us through emotional pain. Some use drugs or alcohol, others use busyness...guess that's what I do. I finished up another course for my PhD while you were sick."

"How will we prevent this from happening again? Did Dr. Paul have any ideas?"

"Guess we didn't discuss that specifically, but he does think we need to get to the bottom of the dream–nightmare, I'd call it–that set me off last time. Oh, Lee..." his eyes threatened to spill again, "if I could just undo all the hurt.... I can hardly believe you came to look after me when I deserted you...."

"My darling Brett...Sweetheart...we need to put this behind us and move on. I think I'm feeling comfortable again...in our relationship, I mean. Besides, they've found the source of my illness and I'm feeling better than I have in a long time. Let's trust the Lord together; can we do that?"

He pulled her into his arms and held her close. "I don't know what I did to deserve you. Guess the Lord knows how much I need you," he whispered.

"How much we need each other," she smiled, and snuggled into his warmth.

She could feel his heart pounding as he held her.

"Do you need me, too, Kitten?"

"*Kitten*, you haven't called me that in a long time." She looked up as his lips sought hers.

"Didn't think I was allowed," he managed between kisses.

She struggled to loosen his arms, "Stop it, Brett Walker."

"No, I'm not going to stop it. And it's not *Brett Walker;* a few moments ago it was *sweetheart* and *darling*...remember that, okay?"

"All right, darling, but we need to talk to the doctor before we...."

"I'm not going to ask a psychologist if I can make love to my wife," he responded emphatically.

"Of course not...I didn't mean him...I mean the ones in charge of your lung...and your other...." his kisses stopped her in mid-sentence.

"You know that I'm okay."

"I know no such thing...*Sweetheart,* " she added.

"Then why don't you call and ask?"

"Because it's after five."

"Our family doctor will still be there...and he'll have all the evidence."

"You certainly are a rascal, Brett Walker."

"But you love rascals," he smirked.

"Just this one," she pushed him away as she reached for the phone.

His smirk continued while she waited for the doctor. He enjoyed putting her on the spot; the question was a delicate one.

After an exchange of pleasantries, she explained, "Brett would like to move back into the master bedroom, and I am wondering whether he's well enough."

He could hear the doctor chuckle. "My dear Mrs. Walker. You underestimate both the male libido and determination. He won't feel any pain!"

"You're both rascals," she said as he swept her into his arms.

"See," he planted a kiss on her nose as she slowly drifted off, "I told you I didn't forget *everything!*"

CHAPTER TWENTY-NINE

"You really do get more beautiful every day," he smiled as he lay watching her nightly ritual. Her hair shone with each stroke of the brush and fell in a silky wave about her shoulders.

"When did you decide to let it grow long?"

"Don't think I decided. I was just too sick to do anything about it...and it grew. When I started back at the U, I wanted to look as unlike the Leanne I had been before...I didn't want anybody to recognize me...because of the Hencken thing, so I kept it long."

"You are a beautiful woman...in every way."

"Thank you, Sweetheart. Tell me, how did your doctor's appointment go today?"

"Fit as a fiddle. He thinks I should exercise more...maybe we could go walking again, like we used to."

"I'd love to...it's getting to be so nice in the park."

"And I talked to him about a vasectomy."

"A what?" The brushing stopped and she moved to perch on the side of the bed. "Did you say a vasectomy?"

He nodded.

"We haven't even discussed this, Brett. You can't just go ahead...we need to pray...."

"Well, I haven't really *gone ahead*. Anyway, why ever not?"

"Because your body belongs to me, too, remember. It's not just yours to do with as you choose. You know what it says in Corinthians...."

"Fine," he said, reaching for the Bible on the head board. "Show me."

"I'm not exactly sure where to find it," she skimmed through the first chapters of Corinthians. "Yes, here it is:

The husband should fulfill his marital duty to his wife, and likewise the wife to her husband. The wife's body does not belong to her alone but also to her husband. In the same way, the husband's body does not belong to him alone, but also to his wife.
Do not deprive each other.... (I Cor: 7:3-5)

"So," she looked up triumphantly.
"So what?"
"So I have a say in what you do, don't I?"
"Lee, Kitten...I know how you hated being on the pill. And I don't want you to get pregnant...I don't want you to go through that again."
He noticed the blood drain from her face. "What do you mean by that? You don't want *children?*"
"I don't want to lose you, Lee. You nearly died last time."
"I was an undiagnosed, untreated celiac."
"And now you think you're all better?"
"Of course–as long as I stay off gluten."
"And you don't think it will interfere with a pregnancy?"
"I'm sure it won't."
"No...Lee...Kitten...I can't let you do this. The doctor is arranging for...."
"Well, my love, all I can say is that you should have put a little more thought into it before you exercised your conjugal rights...to say nothing of *libido and male determination*," she dragged it out, with a slight smile.
"What do you mean by that?"
"I'm pregnant, Brett."
"How could that be?" he stammered.
"I can't imagine! She chuckled. "You'll just have to figure it out."
"I...I guess I thought you were on the pill."
"Why would I be?"

"Never really gave it any thought."

"Well, you don't need to give it any now either. Besides, I've been feeling so good that you couldn't even tell the difference...no morning sickness. And..." she crawled into bed beside him, "when we have a healthy baby this time, we'll both want to try again?"

"I love you, Mrs. Walker," he murmured against her cheek. "I didn't think I could ever be this happy...a gorgeous wife–who loves me! And a baby! We're going to have a baby! And you're healthy. Oh, Kitten, we need to thank God"

"Indeed we do!"

She loved the way he poured out his heart to the Lord. *What a special man you have given me.*

"Are you as happy with me as I am with you?"

"Mmmmmhm!"

CHAPTER THIRTY

"I forgot to tell you that your brother called me at the office this morning?" she mentioned as they sat over lunch at The Seven Dwarfs.

"James called?...and he didn't want to talk to me?"

"He didn't know you were there; guess he didn't realize your memory had returned. I didn't want to disturb your meeting or I would have transferred his call. Anyway, he wondered if it would be okay to drop by, so I invited him for supper?"

"Are you okay with that, Kitten? You will have put in a full day already...."

"I thought maybe you'd barbeque some ribs...keep it simple. He's wanting fellowship with big brother more than anything. He mentioned some pictures of his mom and dad–your mom and dad–and you, and I agreed he should bring them along."

"Wow! That will be something. I never got a thing from home. I wonder what Rosita did with all our personal stuff?"

"It sounds as though your mom may have left some things for you with the Walls. It will be interesting to see what James brings with him. He seemed anxious to come...especially since you're able to remember his visit at the office. Actually, he was really excited!"

"There's so much of my childhood that I can't really get a grip on...gaps in my memory that Paul Hayes thinks must be blocked-out pain. Don't know if I can face it even now."

"Well, you remember Rosita marrying your dad when he was too sick to know or care...and her son bullying you. You remember that she sent you off to a group home...and the abuse there. Do you think there could be even more...?" She broke off at the look on his face.

"There has to be something to make me numb out the way I did."

"We can face it together, Sweetheart. Just don't leave me out in the cold, okay?"

"That's not an option...I'm committed to keeping in touch with reality...most of all–my special girl," he took her hand across the table.

"I had the strangest thing happen this morning at the bank," she changed the subject.

He raised an eyebrow and waited for more.

"I met Bev Carter...remember her?"

"Yep!" he smiled.

"And she got all embarrassed. Mentioned that she had a few legal problems to get straightened around...and wondered if I still wanted to see her?"

She found his grin less than amusing.

"So what are you smirking about? Don't you think that's a little strange? After all, she was my client for nearly two years...we did her dad's estate...then her husband's.... Whatever is so amusing?"

"Well, it's not a big deal, but...well...she tried to date me when we were separated. Guess she heard some gossip and decided to cash in on it."

"Oh my! Oh my! So what happened?"

"Nothing. I remember telling her you were studying in Toronto...that I was married and intended to stay that way. She left very embarrassed and hasn't called since. Course we were long done with the estate...I had been wondering why she continued to make appointments...." he stopped at the look on her face.

"So?"

"So what?"

"So what do I do now...what would you like me to do?"

"What did you leave her with this morning?"

"I told her to make an appointment and come in."

"Nothing wrong with that. I don't intend to alienate her. She was a good client...kept her appointments...paid her bills. I doubt she'll mention the incident but if she does...."

"Thanks for cluing me in," she rose to go. "By the way, speaking of Toronto–I need to spend at least a week there this month. I'll be glad to see the end of this semester."

"You're not going alone–you know that!"

"Are you asking...or telling?"

"Telling." He raised an eyebrow to press home his point. "You're not going to Toronto alone as long as Hencken is loose and on the prowl. Dave and I definitely agree on that point."

"Anything else that I should know about?"

"I'll be going with you," then raising his hands at the expected challenge, he added, "and don't even think otherwise. Besides, you're the one who reminded me that your body belongs to me too. You might say I intend to protect my rights." The corner of his mouth turned up in that confident grin...he had won that round!

She smiled.

"Come on...come on...say it!"

"Say what?"

"You mean you forgot your favourite line?"

"My line?" she feigned innocence.

"Yeah! 'You're a rascal, Brett Walker'," he mimicked her tone.

"No need. We both know!"

CHAPTER THIRTY-ONE

She enjoyed watching the easy comradery between the brothers...happy that they had found each other after all these years...thrilled that they were catching up on the past.

"Why don't we just clear this table?" Brett suggested, as James brought out the treasures to share with his brother. And treasures they were!

"I guess you know that both of my moms were best friends," he looked at Brett.

"If I knew, I can't remember. Mom Wall does look familiar though. My folks' wedding album! Wow! I haven't seen that since before Mom died." He leafed through the pages...noting the lovely young bride...her hair like a golden crown beneath her veil....and his father in a pin-stripe suit...even on his wedding pictures he was austere. He found himself wondering why she had married him.

"That's my mom–I mean Mom Wall," the younger brother interjected. "She was our birth-mom's attendant...maid of honour, or whatever. Course that's not Dad Wall standing with Dad Walker...don't know who that is."

Brett was speechless as they leafed through a family album...pictures of him since he was born...at the swimming pool– taking lessons...playing soccer...a birthday party. Several snapshots showing very clearly that his mom was pregnant. Very few pictures of his dad...course he couldn't remember him being there most of the time.

"Is there anything you can share with me about my mom and dad...things the Walls may have mentioned?"

"Well, they've shared quite a bit since they told me about my big brother," he smiled. I'm not sure what you'd like to know. Guess you must know that Dad Walker was an abuser?" He stopped as the blood drained from Brett's face. "Sorry, maybe you didn't know...."

"Oh, my!" Leanne gasped, then held her breath. James stopped...his mouth open in mid-sentence. Both looked at Brett...his eyes stared–unseeing...his face ghastly white.

O God, his wife prayed, *Please help...I think Brett's in shock.* She looked at James; he was watching his big brother very closely.

"Are you all right, Brett?" he ventured.

He seemed neither to hear nor understand, but stared off into the distance; his mind in another world.

They both jumped as Leanne screamed, "Brett, stop that! Stop that at once! Don't you dare numb-out on me!"

He looked at her for a moment as though she was a stranger, then shaking his head he apologized, "Sorry...sorry...guess that explains some things." He lapsed into silence, shaking his head from time to time.

"So, your folks–the Walls–they knew he was an abuser?"

"Yes...Dad–that is Dr. Wall– was her doctor. Apparently, they had a child on the way when they married. They didn't know if Dad Walker resented having to marry, or if he was just an abuser, but he beat her until she lost it. She would never admit that he did; she always claimed her bruises were from falling...."

"That fills in a lot of blanks for me. I remember Mom being pregnant a couple of times. She would be all white and sick and bruised; she'd go to the hospital and come home without a baby."

"You don't remember him beating her? Leanne asked.

Again he sat silently...his eyes blank.... "I remember waking in the night and hearing her scream...one night she crept into bed with me. Wait...wait...I remember something else...O God, no...no. Before that happened...before she slept with me, I mean...I heard him yelling, and she screamed, 'no Barton...no...you'll kill us both.' Then I heard him hit her and I jumped out of bed and ran to their bedroom. He was beating her with his belt...with the buckle end. I screamed and ran to her. He threw me on the floor and stood over me with the belt. I don't know why he didn't beat me...then he ordered me back to bed and told me to stay there...and to keep my mouth shut or I'd get worse than that."

His brother's face showed both horror and sympathy. "How old were you, Brett?"

"I can't remember...I was in school...maybe grade one or two. Guess I numbed it out–I never thought of it again...until now."

James nodded. "Mom Wall told me that he wanted her to abort whenever she got pregnant. She refused and he beat her till she miscarried. I think she left him when she was carrying you...don't know why she went back after you were born. Guess he cried and made promises...he was a very troubled man...and she was a very kind-hearted woman. She lost two more but wouldn't admit she was being beaten."

"How come you escaped, James?" Leanne asked.

"My folks think he was already well on the way with Lou Gehrig's Disease and needed her care. He may have been unable to do much damage any more. Mom Walker approached my folks to adopt me, and of course they were thrilled–who wouldn't be?" he spread out his hands and grinned.

He even grins like Brett, Leanne decided.

"Did she ever admit that he beat her?"

"Apparently on her death bed. She admitted it all to Mom Wall. It was too late to do anything about it...he was too weak to hurt you, and too sick to marry again. They just left it unreported."

Leanne turned to Brett, "So he never beat you? or did you just numb it out?"

"Don't think he ever really beat me. He just ignored me...sort of like I wasn't there. The pictures bear that out...he's simply not there."

Her eyes filled with tears as she remembered the fun times with her dad...the games... camping trips...family nights... cuddling with him...watching the Blue Jays, the Maple Leafs.... Brett had none of that...yet he loved to play with Mandy.... *You've given me one incredible man, Lord. Help us to be the kind of family you want us to be.*

He lay in bed watching her brush her hair. "I know what happened the night I moved out of our bedroom."

"You do?" She put the brush aside and perched on the side of the bed, her eyes wide.

He nodded. "It just came to me. I had this horrible nightmare...with beating and screaming...and when I woke I was standing over you with a belt. I don't know how it happened...it was like...like I was somebody else...somehow I had turned into...Dad!"

She looked at him...her eyes enormous.

"Guess I knew enough to get out of there before I hurt you. I don't recall when I suddenly went numb."

"Oh, Brett...oh, my poor darling...how awful for you...all these years!" she paused. "Do you think that's the thing that has plagued you–terrorized you–all this time?"

"I do! It was the missing piece of the puzzle. Poor James! Guess I shocked him pretty good...no worse than he shocked me...a rude awakening. I wonder what Dr. Paul will think of this?"

"Maybe we can see him when we go in next month."

"Good idea...should be interesting."

"Did you intend to tell your brother about our baby?"

"Yeah, I was all excited about it...then when we heard about Dad...and what he did to Mom when she was pregnant...I...I guess I thought...I don't know...it just didn't seem the right time."

"I agree with you, dearest; there'll be another time...hopefully happier circumstances."

He touched the lamp, then drew her close, "I love you, Mrs. Walker...I love you."

"Mmmmmhmm," she murmured softly.

CHAPTER THIRTY-TWO

The inscription on the small white tombstone was beautifully etched:

Merri-Lee Walker
April 15, 2000
Infant daughter of Brett and Leanne Walker
Safe in the arms of Jesus.

Tears flowed freely as they stood by the small grave. The tiny rosebush was showing signs of life.

"She would have been a year old today," Leanne snivelled. "She would have been such fun...like Mandy."

He nodded and pulled her close as he mopped his own tears.

"Do you suppose she's having fun with her grandpa and grandma...both grandpas and grandmas?"

"Guess I'd never considered that aspect. A wonderful thought...I never really thought about my dad being in heaven."

"Was he a believer?"

He pondered a few moments, "Yeah, I think so...just never could admit his failings and get help. Guess he passed that on without any effort on his part."

"God has been good to us, my darling...given us a second chance. And I want to believe our wee angel will be rejoicing with us...as will Mom and Dad. And your folks, too. Your dad will be perfect...."

She looked at him and they shared a smile through their tears.

"Tell me something, Lee," he began as they walked back to the car. "Didn't we have a crib, and clothes and stuff for the baby last time? I couldn't find anything to dress her in."

"Of course, we did. I had it all sent to Toronto...to the condo. I intended to head to Toronto within the month to give birth. But I did have things for her in the bag that I packed for the hospital...guess you never noticed it when you were looking for her things. It was in the master bedroom rather than the nursery."

He nodded. "Did you like what we got for her? Dave and I shopped...."

"Yes. It was just right...and I think it was good...I mean...I know it was hard for you, but maybe it was good for you to feel like you had a part...a father's role...." she stopped, not quite sure where she was going with this.

"You may be right. The Lord allowed me to accept responsibility...way too late...way too little...but I think it may have helped with my grief."

"We need to get some breakfast."

"Want to try that little place on Wellington?"

"Sounds good to me."

"I'm glad it's Saturday...we've been needing some unscheduled time together before I head into the lions' den next week," she smiled across the table as they waited for breakfast.

"I'll be in the den with you," he responded, "and I don't expect to be more than a few yards away while you study. I intend to be your knight in shining armour...after all, I have two to protect now."

"Are you forgetting that Hencken isn't allowed anywhere near the university or anywhere that students congregate?"

"No, but he's no longer being monitored. It wouldn't take much for him to slip in...."

"You really don't think he'll try anything, do you? I mean...I'll either be in the classroom or in my study carrel in Bora Laskin. By the time he finds out where I am...."

"I'll be there, Leanne. You've made the Bora Laskin Library your study habitat for years...he'll know exactly where you are. And...he knows you're working on your masters'. How much trouble would it be to keep track of the weeks you come?...you're a bearcat for scheduling...he knows your habits...."

"Guess you're right about that...on all counts. He'll also know that grad students get to use the private study carrels–the one's for lap tops, I mean."

"You'd better arrange for something that allows me to settle in close proximity...you're not getting out of range...."

"Honestly, sweetheart! What could he possibly do?"

"Kitten," he reached for her hand across the table, "I've messed up enough times...neither of us can afford...." he looked down to hide the sudden sting of tears. Then gaining control, his determined blue eyes met her questioning green ones, "So let me do this for both of us–all three of us."

"All right, my love, we'll just go with whatever you think is best," her eyes were soft and warm as she smiled and squeezed his hand.

CHAPTER THIRTY-THREE

He smiled as he admired himself in the full-length mirror.... Yes! Yes! Yes! His new image would do very nicely...no one would take a second look; he could easily pass for a grad student. The beige turtleneck covered the splotchy red birthmark...the sleeve looked after the one on top of his left hand–course nobody would recognize him by now; most of the students he knew had graduated....

The smile turned to an ugly sneer as his thoughts centred on the intended target–he'd get her...no question about that! Too bad he didn't get her that night in her condo...he nearly had her...then she kicked and disabled him–he could still feel the pain when he remembered–and the bulldozer of a boyfriend showed up...and the cops! Well, she wouldn't have any protection this time...she wouldn't even know who he was until...until...it was too late! He could do what he came to do at a moment's notice...didn't need a lot of time...just needed to get her alone...and when he was done even the lawyer wouldn't be able to have her.

Too bad I didn't get her pregnant, he mused, *that would have fixed her, the little witch...taping my messages...calling the cops...giving evidence...getting me ten years in the slammer. Well, I'm not down yet...I still have an appeal coming up...I'll be out permanently ...and in the meantime....*

He checked his image one more time...dark brown wig–well past his collar, beard trimmed and dyed brown...moustache–a bit sparse but the grey had been touched up to match his beard....levis, turtleneck, tweed sport coat.... *I should have done this 20 years ago,* he decided...*makes me look ten years younger.* Yes, definitely, he

152

looked like any other grad student. It would be a cinch to get into the library. He grinned and winked at himself in the mirror before he picked up his computer, tucked it in his backpack, and headed to Bora Laskin Law Library. She would be in today–*that* he could depend on!

CHAPTER THIRTY-FOUR

"It just happened so fast," Aunt Maude Davis sobbed as she stood beside the hospital bed. "One minute we were discussing the newscast and the next he just slumped over the arm of the chair–you know, his favourite one–and I ran to him and...and...and..." she dissolved in tears as Leanne placed an arm around her shoulders.

"I wish you had called sooner, Aunt Maude," Brett stood on the other side of the bed, "I'm sorry you had to go through this alone. Have you talked to the doctor since his initial examination?"

"Yes, he's been in and out several times. They've taken blood tests and arranged for a scan of some sort...MRI, I think he said. He thinks it's a stroke...."

"Uncle Ben," Brett leaned over the old judge as his eyes flickered. "Can you hear me, Uncle Ben?" He continued to talk though the patient showed no signs of recognition.

"Have you called Dave and Sherry?" The older lady shook her head. "Well, I'll just slip out and give them a call. Sherry will call her mom and dad. We don't want to leave you here alone, Auntie; we'll arrange for one of us...." Brett nodded in agreement.

"I don't want to leave him here alone...he wouldn't like that," Aunt Maude's voice was tearful. "Do you think they'd let me stay with him...you know...like you did with Brett?"

"We'll certainly find out," Leanne replied as she headed toward the door. "I'll make some enquiries after I call Dave."

"I'm sure they'll get you a couch or a recliner, Aunt Maude, but we can take turns at night. No need for you to exhaust yourself. There are enough of us to look after both of you," Brett gave her a warm hug.

"That's so sweet of you...I know we're not really family...."

"Well, we don't know how *family* could be any more real. You just let us look after you like you've always looked after us."

She jumped as the old judge muttered imperceptibly. "I'm here, my love, I'm here," she soothed, gently running her fingers through his hair. His hand moved as if he heard, but his eyes remained closed. "And Brett is here with us, dear, and Leanne has gone to call Dave."

"Sherry and Dave will be right along...as soon as they drop Mandy at her folks," Leanne smiled as she came through the door. "I brought you a little sandwich and a salad from Tim Horton's, Aunt Maude. How long has it been since you've eaten?"

"I don't know, dear. I guess we had just finished breakfast when..." her eyes filled with tears.

"Come," Leanne led her gently to the chair and arranged her supper on a tray.

"So good of Dave and Sherry to stay with Auntie for a while. I'm about starved," Leanne commented as they sat over supper at the hospital cafeteria.

"I know you're eating for two, but...do you really intend to eat all that?"

"Just watch me! He does away with it as fast as I get it to him."

"So it's a *him*?"

"No girl would eat like that, besides...he's starting to kick like a quarterback."

They smiled companionably at one another as he took her hand and returned thanks for the meal.

"I really don't think it would be right for me to trot off to Toronto and just leave Aunt Maude. What do you think?"

"Well...I wondered how long it would take you to come to that conclusion. I gather that Dave and Sherry, and Sherry's parents would not be deemed sufficient back-up?" He looked at her questioningly.

"You *gathered* correctly. Why don't I wait another couple of days and see how Uncle Ben comes around. I think she'll be fine once he can communicate. She's so afraid he'll leave her...afraid of being alone."

"I understand that, Kitten, but I don't want you to miss your classes."

"Guess I'll just get them by e-mail," she made a face, "and do my research on the Web. If all goes well, we can leave Wednesday."

He nodded. "I'm planning to stay with Ben tonight."

"You?"

"Definitely not you."

"Why ever not? I'm all practised...I know how to get the most out of that excuse for a bed."

"Not any more. There's more of you now, and besides, both of you need your sleep."

"You are something else, Brett Walker!"

"Can we just try that again? *You are something else, Sweetheart!* he grinned.

CHAPTER THIRTY-FIVE

He breathed a sigh of relief as he sauntered past the young man at the information desk. *Guess I can still pass for a student–he scarce gave me a glance,* he thought derisively. It rankled him that he could no longer flaunt the *Doctor Hencken, Professor of Law* image. He owed *her* for that, and she would pay...maybe even today. He fondled the pouch on his backpack–it was there–loaded and ready.

*Wonder what she's driving...I didn't see the purple thing in the parking lot...course it wasn't at the condo either...she might be using the Jetta...it wasn't in the driveway this morning ...course it isn't here either...*he mused as he sauntered from floor to floor in search of his victim. *Can't believe she's not in her usual spot...unless of course she no longer studies at Bora Laskin. If she has any virtue at all, it would be dependability. I'll just hang around a while...no need to rush off...I have my computer...my favourite web site will help get me fired up....*

His temper got the best of him as noon hour approached and his plans went awry. *What a waste...one more thing she'll pay for...keeping me waiting....* He fingered the pouch. *I wonder if this will keep in the fridge...better not take a chance...I'll reload tomorrow.*

He swore as his fingers twitched nervously. He would have to watch that...someone might notice...ask questions...recognize his voice. He swore again as he jammed them into his pockets.

The vigil continued. It was now past lunch hour...he would need to eat...that meant the cafeteria...he may have to say something...someone might recognize...course he could go off campus...but then he might miss her. The jacket and long-sleeved sweater were heavier than he anticipated. He muttered an oath as he wiped at the perspiration on his forehead. *Blasted wig...never realized it would be itchy. Guess I'd better get out of here and rip it off.*

While he waited for his burger and fries at McDonald's, he spied the Jetta. It was in the line ahead of him. He watched as it pulled slowly into the parking lot and stopped. Well...he would just do the same...from a safe distance of course. He congratulated himself on choosing McDonald's–Leanne's favourite watering hole; he knew it...just knew it...sooner or later she would show up. He wondered if she was alone...blast those darkened windows...he couldn't see how many were in the car...not her car...must be Brett's...always parked at the condo. Maybe today was his lucky day after all...he may not have to go through all this torture one more day!

His stomach reacted as he gulped the burger and fries, trying desperately to wash it down with the coke. He'd have to slow down...can't throw up here...attract too much attention. He choked as it caught in his throat. He grabbed the paper bag and struggled to relieve himself of the offending blockage.

He reached again for the coke, then noticed the Jetta had moved. There it was...just turning left out of the parking lot.... His stomach lurched again and he reached for the bag while trying to keep track of the sleek vehicle ahead of him. His hand missed the bag and the coke emptied into his lap...the offending meal would not be contained and it came to rest on the front of his jacket and shirt. Swearing loudly, he wiped at the sweat that poured down his face and clouded his eyes.

No matter, he assured himself as he swung out of the parking lot....*today's the day...today she would pay...and maybe even Brett with her!*

The Jetta didn't seem to be heading to the library...no matter...he would just follow...it had to stop somewhere. He chuckled to himself as he followed as closely as he dared. No matter if they saw him now...they'd never recognize him...his mom's old car. If only he knew who was in there...and how many...it would remove a little of the uncertainty.

His pulse quickened as his prey turned into an unfamiliar parking lot. No one noticed the plain grey Volvo pull in behind. He'd bide his time....no need to rush now and complicate matters. He reached for his backpack...his weapon ready.

The door of the Jetta was opening...now was his big moment...he tried to extricate himself from the seat belt which he had neglected to unlock...his weapon fell to the floor and expunged its contents. He watched as a blonde, well-built, athletic male in cut-offs swung his backpack over his shoulder and headed into the Engineering building.

He fell heavily back on the seat; his world–spinning wildly out of control–spiralled downward into nothingness.

CHAPTER THIRTY-SIX

"You've just got to help me, Leanne... you're my only hope!"

Recognizing her caller, Leanne hesitated with her hand on the nob. "Whatever are you doing at my door at this hour of the night...in the rain?" she asked the bedraggled woman.

"Please let me in...please...please...don't turn me away...."

"Have you run away from the hospital? Do they know you are out?"

"Well...they don't exactly lock me up. I can decide...."

"I'm not going to play games with you, Rhonda. Are you out on a pass? It's after ten o'clock." She reached for the phone.

"No...No...." the shivering woman flung herself across the room. "Please...don't turn me in. I really am allowed out sometimes...just not at night....I can get back in without anyone knowing. I need your help. You offered once...." She stopped as Leanne looked up in surprise.

"That was a long time ago—before you tried to ruin our lives."

"But I'm sorry...so very sorry! I'd never do it again," she sobbed.

"So what has happened to make you sorry? Leanne tried to soften the harshness in her voice.

"All kinds of things. I've had shock treatments...."

Leanne waited.

"Besides...I've had someone visiting me...he believes like you do. He's been counselling me, and....and...."

"And?"

"Well...I know you won't believe this," she paused noting the look of skepticism."

"So...are you trying to tell me that you have come to a knowledge of God...of Christ? Or are you trying to use...?"

"No," she wailed. "You must believe me...I really have asked His forgiveness, but I'm not like you...yet...I mean I...I ...I'm not all, you know...fixed up yet...I'm still learning."

"So, tell me, who is this counsellor? Is he a psychiatrist? A psychologist?"

"No. He's a preacher...pastor...whatever...says he knows you."

"Who might that be?"

"Reverend Somerville."

"Pastor Bill Somerville! From Cornerstone Church?"

"Yeah."

"So how did this come about? How did you get to know him?"

"They asked me to get counselling. I didn't want the shrink...you know what I mean.... They insisted, so I just came up with the pastor's name out of the blue. Don't even know where it came from...I must have heard you use it or...whatever. So I called him and he came."

"And then?"

"He talked to me about Christ...and I was plenty ticked. He told me he was a Christian counsellor...that was what I told the psych's I wanted...to get them off my back. They had to honour my request. So I was stuck with him. But the more he came and the more he talked and showed me stuff in the Bible, the more he made sense.

"Look, I'm soaked to the hide...can I sit by the fire, or have a towel, or...?"

"Of course. I'm sorry." She hurried for a bath towel and showed the dripping girl to the family room. *Guess I should be thankful that Brett is the one staying at the hospital tonight. What if he was here alone?* She pulled her robe closely around her as she seated herself across from Rhonda.

"You look pregnant. Are you pregnant? Brett's baby?"

Leanne noticed the look of overwhelming sadness as she nodded.

"Didn't I hear that you lost one?"

"Yes, we did," Leanne nodded again.

"I...I...I am sorry...you know...that I aborted mine...even if the guy was a jerk. It was like you said...I'd be sorry one day. Pastor Somerville took me through the story of creation and the Psalms, too...where it tells how God created me in my mother's womb and all. I cried...you know...really cried...not pretend tears."

"I'm glad to hear that, Rhonda. I guess I didn't really think you understood the difference between reality and pretense."

"I don't think I did, but it's been almost a year now since I've been in counselling, and I'm learning all kinds of things."

"I'm sure you are,"Leanne smiled warmly. "So what do you want from me?"

"I need a lawyer."

"For?"

"Pastor Somerville thinks I need to get after my dad." She paused at the surprise on Leanne's face.

"Pastor Somerville?"

"Well, he says he needs to be stopped."

"I hadn't realized he was still...."

"Well, he is, and I agree he needs to be stopped."

"Indeed he does, but I am not the one to take your case."

"I guess I'm wondering if you could fix me up with that women's lawyer that Brett told me to see?"

"Did you see her?"

"Well, I did, but we didn't...get on. She knew my reputation and all...and I don't think she believed half of what I told her...so I just...."

"You just what, Rhonda?"

"Gave her a piece of my mind."

"Ouch! She is clearly the best as far as women's advocacy goes. You'll need to apologize before you get another chance."

"I'm prepared to do that...but she won't take my calls...doesn't call back. I know I don't deserve your help, but...."

I can't believe I'm hearing this! from Rhonda! "Well, Rhonda, I will discuss this with Brett, and...."

"No...no...no. You know what he'll say. He hates me."

"I don't think he does, Rhonda, but you have certainly not earned any brownie points. As I was saying, we will discuss it. Now I'm going to call a cab for you," she picked up the phone, "and I want to hear from the staff there that you have returned–through the front door...."

"No...no!" she wailed. "They'll take away my day pass...they'll lock me up."

"As I was saying...you'll go in the front door and take your licks. It will be a good lesson for you."

"And then you'll help me?"

"I didn't say that, Rhonda. I said I would consider it...providing you deal with your mistakes on the up and up–starting tonight. You could have come during the day...made an appointment...sent an e-mail. Tell me...honestly now...did you choose this dramatic entrance to get my sympathy?"

While she hesitated, Leanne reminded her, "I want an *honest* answer."

"Possibly...though I didn't sit down and map it out. It's just...just...."

"Just second nature?"

"Yeah, I guess so," Rhonda chuckled.

"All right, now, Rhonda. If you really are a new believer...if you really want your life to change...you have to start with basic honesty. You should be back at the hospital in less than 30 minutes...I'll wait that long for their call before I go to bed. Is it a deal?"

"A deal," she replied, offering her hand.

The call came as Leanne was slowly drifting off. *Almost midnight*, she yawned as she reached for the phone.

"This is the administrator's office. I want you to know that Rhonda has returned..." she hesitated as someone in the background prompted, "through the front door." The voice continued, "through the front door."

"I'm sorry...I don't believe you gave me your name."

"This is the administrator's office. My name is..." Again the prompt in the background, "Marjory Thornton." She continued, "My name is Marjory Thornton."

Leanne smiled. *Yeah, right! The administrator is still there at midnight!* "Is Rhonda there? Can I talk to her, please?"

"No, she isn't here right now. Can I have her call you in the morning?"

"By all means."

She hung up the phone and dialed the number on the call display. *As I thought, a pay phone. She probably didn't even return to the hospital. The little wretch! Guess I'll just wait for her to call me again. That will be interesting!*

CHAPTER THIRTY-SEVEN

The beam of sunlight forced its way between the draperies and caught the sleeper unaware. *It certainly gets light early now,* she mused, then glanced at the bedside clock.

"Ten o'clock!" she shrieked. "Wonder what happened to Brett...if he came home this morning...why he didn't wake me."

His hastily written scrawl leaned against the bedside lamp. *You looked so peaceful, I couldn't wake you. Meet me for lunch? Love you, Brett Walker.*

She smiled at the *'Brett Walker'. It's a wonder he didn't sign it 'Sweetheart'.*

"So, how was your night? Did you manage to get to sleep in that...?" she asked as they sat over lunch.

He chuckled. "I'm not sure I'd call it *sleep*, but yeah, I'm at least half awake this morning. From the contented noises coming from your side of the bed when I came for a shower..." he stopped as she made a face, "...well I know you don't snore...but whatever it is that you do when you're sleeping...." he laughed, "I didn't have the heart to wake you two."

"You're a rascal, Brett Walker, *Sweetheart.* Tell me, how did Uncle Ben make it through the night?"

"He slept well...didn't even wake when they checked on him...took his vitals and whatever."

"So, is there improvement?"

"Oh, yeah. He's lucid...knows who I am. Asked for Maude."

"Wow! Does he seem to be paralysed?"

"Not that I could discern. Aunt Maude–and Dave...think you should get on with your classes, but..." he stopped in mid-sentence.

"But?"

"Well...my schedule is full; I let Becky book appointments since I would be here anyway...."

"You know Sweetheart...."

"Don't start. You are *not* going without me."

"You're over-reacting, Love. I could stay with Bill and Billie...drive your car...by the time anyone knows I'm there, I'm gone."

"We'll go next week, Leanne." She noticed the determined set of his jaw.

"Really, Brett!"

"So you think I'm overbearing?" It was more like a question than a statement.

She smiled. "I know you love me, Dearest. I think perhaps I would call it a little over-caring."

"I do love you, Kitten. I can't bear the thought that maybe Lonnie...." sudden tears stung his eyes.

"Fine! I'll come to the office now, then, and finish off the Brigmann estate...unless, of course, you have more pressing matters for me."

"You have quite a number of new files on your plate, but, no matter, I just enjoy knowing you're next door to me. I'm going to enjoy having you back once you're through school. I can hardly wait."

"Aren't you forgetting something?"

"Such as?"

"Walker number three."

"I have it all planned out. We'll just set up a place for him...he may as well get used to the legal atmosphere...jargon. Can't start too soon."

She grinned. "So...I'll have to contend with two rascals!"

"What if it's a girl? What will you say then?"

"This is a boy!"

He grinned and took her hand across the table.

"I almost forgot to tell you that I had a visitor last night."

"A visitor...at night. Who, pray tell?"

"You'd never guess."

"So?"

"Rhonda Fleming?"

"Rhonda? She dared to come to *our house?* Whatever for?"

"She wanted me to help her get an appointment with Brandy...you know the women's advocate, Lucille Brandon."

"That's fine and well, but what was she doing out of the hospital...and at night?"

"Valid questions, my love. She apparently snuck out...though she has a day pass...and expected to sneak back in. I asked her why she came in the rain...soaked and pathetic...and suggested to her that it was a ploy to get my sympathy."

"How did she respond to that?"

"She said she hadn't sat down and planned it, but agreed with me that it came very naturally to her."

"I'll be doggoned! Did you turn her in?"

"No."

"Why not?"

"I was interested in her story. She claims that she has been taking counsel from Bill Somerville and has made a commitment to Christ. Some of the things she shared seemed valid."

"Well, I'll be! I suppose you agreed to help her."

She shrugged her shoulders and raised one eyebrow. "Well, not really...not yet. I said I would think about it only if she went back to the psych hospital through the front door and explained her actions. She was to have the night nurse call and confirm."

"Did she?"

"No. She had a friend call from a payphone and pretend she was the administrator, Marjory Thornton. I was too amused to be angry."

"So what now? Did you check her story with Bill?"

"I called him this morning. He confirmed that he has been seeing her for almost a year, and she has made a commitment to Christ. I agreed with him that she has changed a great deal...a long way to go.

Actually, she mentioned that she is still learning."

"Honestly, Kitten, you are something else. You know you should have turned her in."

"Everybody deserves a second chance...."

"A second chance! How about ninety-fifth?"

"Come now, Dearest. Where would we be if everyone had given up on us...if we had given up on each other?"

His gaze was warm, "My little social worker."

"I'm thankful I was home last night instead of you."

"Rhonda had better be thankful, too," he grinned.

CHAPTER THIRTY-EIGHT

He was wet and cold and a putrid smell assaulted his nostrils. *Another one of those wretched dreams,* he swore. He tried to roll over to ease his misery, then found himself caught in a restraint of some sort. It took a few minutes to realize where he was...in a car...in the middle of the night...and the smell.... He swore again as the memory of the afternoon surfaced. Thankfully, no one had reported him...called security...or worse–called an ambulance. He took stock of himself. The seat belt was tangled around his shoulder and right arm...his wig had slipped down his *forehead–good thing it didn't cover my face...I could have smothered...*he had escaped detection by the law–not that he worried all that much about having no licence– his dad would look after the charges–it was just that he was parked on forbidden ground...he would pay a high price for being on the university grounds. Still...he felt better than he did in the afternoon ...perhaps the cold had revived him, he thought, even as he shivered.

The shadow on the window caught his attention as the motor began to purr. More oaths erupted as he snatched the offending ticket from beneath the wipers. One more thing to add to his list of grievances...*she'll pay...you just bet she'll pay...for the rest of her life...if she survives at all!*

The old man will be his outrageous self; let him rant and rave...there's really nothing else he can do to me. He grimaced as he punched in the security code. As the interior light came on in the spacious garage, he looked at himself–he was a mess. Oh, well, he would just stuff this jacket and shirt...too warm anyway. He would sleep in, shop for something more suitable to the weather. Not likely his dad would notice the mess in the car. He would leave a note for the butler....

One thing for sure, he promised himself as he drifted toward sleep...*I'll have to work smarter. Just keep track of the condo...I'll not go to the library until I know she's there. That will simplify things....*

"A lady would like to talk to you," Melva informed her as she touched her intercom.

"A lady? We don't have a name?"

"She says to call her *no name*, but she sounds like Rhonda trying to disguise her voice."

"Put her through," Leanne chuckled.

"Is this Leanne?"

"Yes, Rhonda. Why are you calling me?"

"To apologize for last night...for trying to deceive you."

"Well, I'll be!" She listened for a moment, then asked, "Rhonda, are those real tears or some of your theatrics?"

"I'm sorry. I didn't really mean to cry. They're real, but I'm not trying to manipulate you. I was just too scared to do what you said last night, but I know I did wrong. I have gone to the administration and confessed...and they've grounded me and taken away my day pass."

"Good! It's time you faced the consequences of your actions. Why are you calling me?"

"I...guess...I hoped...you would forgive me if I tried to make it right...and maybe you would help me...anyway."

"I could call Brandy on your behalf, but how would you get to see her if you can't get a pass? You seem to have shot yourself in the foot."

"I know...I know...but I am trying to do right."

Leanne was suddenly overwhelmed with sympathy for this girl, who had been through so much pain...had caused so much pain to so many others. *Who knows what she might have become if she would have had some guidance...a positive role model...besides she is a child of God...albeit a struggling one.*

"Tell you what, Rhonda, I'll call Brandy and have a chat. We'll leave the results in God's hands. That's all I can do. In the meantime, you need to be asking God for guidance and direction in your life, and in this situation with your dad."

"Oh, I have been, and thank you...thank you...thank you. I know I don't deserve your help."

This really is a new Rhonda, she mused...*she'll need more help than I can give her...maybe I'll call Pastor Bill and see if they have someone in 'Community Care' that might be able to come alongside....*

CHAPTER THIRTY-NINE

"I'm sorry to disturb you, Mr. Hencken, sir," the elderly butler stepped timidly into the den and addressed his employer; "but I perceive, sir, that Mr. Hencken Jr., that is Professor Hencken does not appear to be at all well."

"Good morning, Morgan. Not well, you say? Why would you think that?"

"He left me this note, sir, asking me to tidy his car, but it does appear that he has been ill...to the point of losing his supper, sir, and there is a very disturbing item on the floor...sir...."

He stopped at the look of anguish on the lawyer's face. "Describe *disturbing*, Morgan."

"Well, sir...I'm not sure, sir...it rather appears to be a hypodermic needle of some sort, sir, with blood...." Again he stopped...fidgeted...as though unable to believe what he had seen. "And then, sir, I found this...." He produced the ticket fearfully, as though he himself were responsible.

Staring at the ticket, the senior Hencken barely contained the oath that caught in his throat. "Thank you, Morgan; perhaps he is more ill than I realized. I take it he is still in bed?"

"Indeed, sir. It was well past midnight...."

His employer nodded. I shall look into it at once."

"Shall I clean the car, sir?"

"Allow me to check it first, Morgan, then I shall be much obliged...."

He rose slowly from behind his desk. So Lonnie had violated his parole...had deliberately gone to the university...parked one of the

172

Hencken vehicles for everyone to see...and gotten a ticket as proof of his deed. How like him to flaunt himself in the face of the law. He wasn't sure which grieved him the most...the loss of five hundred grand, or loss of face. Clearly, it was time for another chat with his old friend, Inspector Brighton.

The stench assaulted him as he opened the door of the Volvo. *His wife's car...good thing she didn't live to see what became of her pampered puppy...she'd be heart broken. I aught to make him clean this up...how dare he leave his mess for poor old Morgan. So, he's ill. He certainly doesn't look good...hasn't for some time. I wonder where the needle came from...and whose blood. Better let the inspector take a look at this.*

"Shall I tidy it, sir?" the faithful butler hovered over his shoulder.

"Please do, Morgan, but leave the item there on the floor. I'll need to check this out before we clean it away.

Eleven o'clock found him in earnest conversation with Inspector Graham Brighton.

"We have been keeping an eye on him as you suggested, Gil, and we are aware that he has broken his parole a number of times. His latest disguise is beyond belief...he's becoming quite ingenious...."

"Oh, yes, he's that all right. What do you make of his violations? I take it you...."

"We believe he's after the girl...Leanne Stevenson-Walker. The under-cover boys found him parked behind a Jetta; it belongs to an engineering student who lives in her condo."

"That is disturbing...most disturbing! Why don't you just pick him up?"

"We want to wait until he crosses the line...proves himself incapable of rehabilitation...we don't want to go through all this again in a year or so when some psychiatrist...."

"What if he succeeds with the girl...harms her in some way?"

"We're committed to making sure that doesn't happen?"

"What do you make of the needle...the blood?"

"Don't know. He may have been trying to give himself an injection of some sort and got it wrong. We'll know more once the lab boys do their analysis...we'll know if the blood is his...check it against his DNA."

"What do you think he intends to do to the girl?"

"Don't know that either. He may be just watching...trying to formulate a plan. He very nearly succeeded in his last attempt."

The senior Hencken nodded. "I should have guessed his behaviour was contrived. I wonder if he had the psychiatrist fooled, too, or...."

"What are you thinking?"

"I'm not sure. Just wish I had known a little more about his mind-set before the bail hearing, but he was so determined to go ahead...it came up so fast. Could have saved all of us a lot of grief if we'd known. Guess that's water under the bridge."

"No question about that. We'll do all we can, as you know, to keep him from hurting himself or anyone else. We'll keep an eye on the girl when she comes. Actually, we expected her yesterday...guess Lonnie did, too. I wish we had some way of knowing when she'll show. She usually comes the last week of the month."

"Do I take it she knows nothing of this?"

The inspector nodded, "And she won't if we're successful. I doubt her husband will let her come on her own. I understand he's very protective."

"No surprise there...though he was in quite a terrible accident a few months ago, and wasn't able to be at the bail hearing. He's a formidable opponent. He brought the class-action suit against Lonnie, if you remember. Cleaned him out financially."

The inspector nodded.

"I still find it hard to believe that a man with all the opportunities...." his voice trailed off.

"Wish I could predict what he intends to do this time."

"Don't we all!"

"He'd hardly be foolish enough to try strangling...." They both chuckled remembering how she had kicked him in the groin and disabled him last time. "She's well able to look after herself...quite athletic, I think. And Lonnie...well...he's not strong...lost a lot of weight...seems to have something wrong with him."

CHAPTER FORTY

"So now that we know for sure it's a boy...." he smiled and chanced a look at his wife as they passed Cambridge on their way to Toronto.

"I knew before the ultrasound...I told you it was a boy!"

"So you did...so you did! So...what are we going to name our boy?"

"What are you thinking? Do you want to name him after some of his forebears, or just pick something we like...you know...something meaningful?"

"I think we may have some family members that we like...." he chuckled.

"Don't be a rascal, Brett Walker. Tell me what you have in mind."

"How about your dad, or Dave, or...?"

"I think Dave and Sherry may want to have a little guy in a year or so...better leave *Dave* for them. What about your dad, or your brother? Or maybe the baby's father?" She smiled and squeezed his hand.

"Not my dad."

"What about *Benjamin*, after Uncle Ben? He would be so proud! And my dad's second name is *Benjamin*. I think we should call him after you, too; how about *Benjamin Brett Walker?*"

"I like the *Benjamin*. Uncle Ben will do a flip...he thinks we're his kids anyway, but do you really think we should name him *Brett?*"

"Definitely. Unless you have a second name that I don't know about?"

"It was after my dad; I dropped it as soon as I was old enough to know how. End of discussion."

"All right then,.unless you have other suggestions...we will have a little son named after both his daddy and his grandpa, to say nothing of his adopted uncle." They exchanged a warm smile.

So...there's another black car in the driveway...a black BMW...looks new...must be hers. I knew she'd come sooner or later...wonder what happened to the purple Lexus...maybe she traded it off...or maybe–he hesitated, not wanting to consider the obvious possibility–*unless it's Brett's and he's with her.* It had been a cinch to keep track of the vehicles at the condo; his diligence had paid off. She always leaves early...he'd be watching to make sure it was her...then he'd head home and get loaded. Tomorrow would be the day! His grin turned ugly. *You'll get all that's due you, Leanne Stevenson-Walker!*

"Good meeting?" he asked as they sat over lunch in the cafeteria.

"Excellent! Frank is just the best...I couldn't ask for a better prof or a better faculty advisor. He knows his stuff and really puts out for his students. He had already reviewed what I'd sent in and gave me thumbs up...as well as good suggestions. I appreciate him!"

"I do, too, Kitten. Anybody that appreciates my wife is a friend of mine," he grinned. "So, we're off to Bora Laskin?"

"Sure enough. And yes, I will remember to choose a carrel where my husband can keep an eye on me."

"Don't mock me, Mrs. Walker...you may be glad I'm there."

"I like having you around...even if I don't need you," she quipped.

She couldn't remember seeing the study carrels this full...especially for a summer class. *Wonder what's going on.* She settled in her usual spot, noting the adjacent carrels were already taken; Brett would not be as close as he would like. No matter...all would be well. She glanced at the studious group around her...recognizing no one...then settled into a serious routine.

Try as she might, she could not get over the feeling...someone was watching her. She checked the adjacent carrel...the student was busy at his computer; maybe it was just Brett attempting to keep an eye on her. She tried again to concentrate. Her eyes strayed from time to time to the same student...he *was* a little different...long-sleeved shirt with turtle neck...dark brown hair...maybe a wig, she decided.

By four o'clock her nerves were a frazzle. Having made up her mind, she moved quickly...gathering her notes, closing her computer and slipping it into her backpack. Brett would understand her uneasiness.

"I just couldn't cope. It felt so claustrophobic...like I couldn't breathe properly. Do you think my pregnancy has anything to do with this? Or am I just losing it? Maybe I'm just too old for...."

"Stop it, Kitten. It's none of the above. There were just too many bodies in too close proximity...even I felt a little claustrophobic. Come," he relieved her of the backpack and taking her gently by the elbow, moved her toward the door, "let's just put these in the car and take a brisk walk. A little fresh air will do us both good."

"Honestly, Sweetheart, my nerves are shot. I felt as though someone was watching me, but every time I looked around, no one was."

"Well, I kept a pretty good eye on you," he smiled to reassure her. "Tomorrow we should look for a less congested area...maybe one of those tables where we can sit together."

"Good idea," she agreed, feeling suddenly more relieved than she had all afternoon.

Rats! Another wasted day. She didn't even show till after lunch...wonder if that's going to be a new pattern...and if her guardian angel is going to hover over her all week, or if...if... There has got to be a loop hole somewhere. Wonder if he'll follow her to the washroom...the corridor might be a good place. So...she's pregnant! His self talk slowed as a sly grin escaped. *So...all three will pay!*

His patience had long expired as noon hour approached, and his victim had not arrived. Her carrel remained empty, along with several others. *What's the matter with her? She's always prompt...predictable! She left the house at the usual time...parked in the usual spot. They've got to be in the building. I'll just saunter around....*

Brett was hefting her backpack as he came upon them. Feigning interest in the stacks, he watched as they moved past him toward the main entrance. He noticed that two of the students who had been in the carrels yesterday were now sharing a table downstairs. *No wonder...the air is certainly better here...I'll just join them this afternoon.* He smirked as he quickened his pace...he would just keep an eye on them. If this was a pattern, he may know where to apprehend...perhaps in the parking lot. In his pre-occupation, he neglected to notice the student in the loose-fitting jacket who casually followed him out.

"I'm so glad we moved from the top floor," she commented as they enjoyed lunch in the park. "And bringing our lunch was a really great idea. I can't remember being claustrophobic before...actually I didn't used to notice the other students...once I got involved in my research, I mean. That guy with the long-sleeved turtle neck just gives me the creeps. I swear he was watching me yesterday." She looked up at her husband, "Do you think I'm over-reacting? the pregnancy...?"

"It's okay, Kitten. It doesn't matter if you're over-reacting; I just want you to have a comfortable climate so you can enjoy your studies. You certainly do enjoy studying. It's a joy to watch you at work."

She smiled and squeezed his hand. "I love you Brett Walker," then noticing his raised eyebrow, she added, "sweetheart."

He chuckled and planted a kiss on her forehead. *I wonder if she'd enjoy this so much if she knew the long-sleeved turtle neck followed us?* he wondered.

CHAPTER FORTY-ONE

"Well, hello there, chapie," Brett teased as Ian burst through the door in his usual manner. "Isn't this a bit early for you?"

"Just stopped in for a bite to eat, and to find my wife...I see she has arrived," he chuckled and indicated her backpack hanging on the bannister.

"Sure enough," Leanne smiled, "and she accepted the offer to join us...spaghetti and meat balls."

"Jolly good," he grinned. "But tell me how a celiac gets to eat spaghetti...isn't that made from some kind of wheat?" he joshed.

She nodded. "Probably from Durham. But this spaghetti is made with rice. Brett claims he can't tell the difference."

"I doubt it will stop me from refuelling," he chuckled as his wife slipped in beside him.

"Have you told Brett and Lee what you told me about the other morning?" Liz asked as they enjoyed supper.

"Actually, it had slipped my mind, but I'm glad you reminded me. You know, it's a bit strange," be began, "but I had been noticing this car parked down the block, just under the trees there...where they hang over the curb, and it seemed a bit odd at that hour of the morning...don't know why I noticed it, except that the driver seemed to be waiting fcr someone...reading the newspaper...I couldn't see whether it was a man or a woman."

"How long ago did this happen?"

"Well, I first noticed it last Monday...then a day or two later in the week–maybe Thursday and Friday...then again yesterday...and it was there this morning. It's a dull grey...maybe a Volvo...not terribly new...maybe a '97 or thereabout."

"Is there a pattern? Do you know how long he stays? when he leaves?" Brett questioned.

"Not really. We leave around seven. This was our week to ride with Johnny and Maria...last week they rode with us...saves a bundle on the parking. We leave our Jetta in the garage when we're gone."

"Does this vehicle ever follow you?"

"Don't think so. At least not from here. Though a funny thing happened last Monday. I'm not sure if it was the same vehicle, but a grey Volvo followed me out of McD's–at lunch time you know–and parked behind me when I went to class. Thought he must be waiting for someone ...I mean you don't just pull into someone else's parking space...but when I came out around 4:30 he was still there...had passed out. Must have been drunk...he was a mess...and his hair had slipped down over his eyes...guess it was a wig. I gave security a call as I left."

"There's a student at the library..." she hesitated, not quite sure where she was going with this, "I think he wears a wig...I'm not sure why I think so...but he just gives me the creeps." *Honestly, Leanne, that was dumb think to bring up,* she chided herself.

"It didn't help that the top floor at Bora Laskin was rather congested...students coming out of the woodwork," Brett came to his wife's aid. "Both of us felt rather claustrophobic."

"Guess a few others did, too. They followed us when we moved to the tables...you know... a more open space." Leanne explained. "Then this afternoon, even the one with the wig joined us."

"Do you think he might be the same guy?" Liz wondered.

"I guess anything's possible," Brett gave a nonchalant shrug.

"This was so sweet of you. I'm sorry we have to rush," Liz apologized as they heard their friend's van in the driveway.

"We understand...only too well," Brett volunteered. "Enjoy your evening."

"I'm glad you seem to be enjoying Ian...and Liz, too," she commented as they sipped their coffee in the family room. "I thought there for a while that you didn't really care for him."

He gave her a questioning look.

"Or at least *he* seemed to think so," she explained.

"Well, I guess I would have to admit that I was a bit curt a time or two. After all, he's very attractive...athletic–which I know you admire–not to mention charming, and he was sharing a house with my wife. How was I supposed to know he was married?"

"Oh, my dear! My dear!"

"I'm sorry, Kitten. It didn't seem like you at all...but then you weren't yourself at all, either, and I was beside myself....I even thought he might have bought you the purple car...and...."

"And?" she prompted.

"And I berated myself for not having looked after you better...got you a car..."

"My poor darling! At least that explains why you wouldn't ride in it. You sure gave me an interesting time. Tell, me, why won't you go to McDonald's?"

"That's easy. Our times there have been the stuff that nightmares are made of...I didn't need any more of those."

"Can you explain?"

He contemplated, then, "It seems to me...I'm not sure...but it does seem that whenever we meet there, our relationship is on the verge of disintegration."

She chuckled. "That's quite an explanation. Now I'm more curious than ever."

"I guess...I think you wanted a place with an easy escape. I always knew that our time together would be like fast food–eat and run. You always left me...."

"I'm sorry, Sweetheart, I never would have made that association."

"Can you explain why you always choose to go there?"

"I've never stopped to wonder. Guess it's handy...familiar...easy to get in and out when I'm in a hurry. My study group liked meeting there...it's a friendly place for me. But it's not a big deal...there's not much I can eat at fast-food restaurants anymore. Besides, I don't want Benjamin Brett addicted before he knows what's good for him," she smiled. "We'll find a place we can both enjoy."

"I love you Mrs. Walker," he murmured as he pulled her close.

CHAPTER FORTY-TWO

"Another great class?"

"You bet," she returned his warm smile, and accepted the juice he had picked up for her. They settled in a secluded corner in the student lounge and she continued in a subdued whisper, "I'm really enjoying being here...except for Bora Laskin. Honestly, Brett, I can't put a finger on what the problem is. I feel so antsy...can't get a grip...like my skin is crawling. I think it has something to do with that student...you know? I mean the one with the turtle neck. Yesterday when he joined us at the tables, I caught him glaring at me a time or two...then when his bony fingers started to twitch...he reminded me so much of Lonnie...if I didn't know better...." She paused and looked at her husband.

He hesitated, then met her gaze head on. She gasped as the realization hit her, "It is Lonnie!!" she mouthed. "Oh, Brett! Do you think it's him?"

His further hesitation increased her anxiety. He nodded slowly. "I hoped you wouldn't come to that conclusion."

"Then it is him? That's why I can't go to the washroom by myself?"

"Yes, I'm afraid it's him all right. I talked to the police this morning while you were in class...they put me through to Inspector Brighton...guess his boys have Lonnie under surveillance."

"So what do we do? Shall I change libraries?"

"They would prefer not. He is in violation of his parole, but they don't want to pick him up until he proves how *off the wall* he really is...they want to put him away for life."

"Oh, my! The poor man! He really is bad off...."

"That will do, Leanne," his voice was gruff. "You're not playing social worker on this one. They're convinced he's out to get you...big time...better you stay where they can protect you."

"So how are they doing that?"

"Under cover. You know the two students in the baggy jackets?"

"Don't tell me. They look like kids."

"On purpose. Part of the cover. They are apparently very skilled...though not sure what he intends to do to you...they're more than capable of taking him down. His father is also very uneasy and has hired a shadow for Lonnie...so altogether we're surrounded by spy and counter spy. You noticed how everybody moved from the carrels when we did...if you wouldn't have been so absorbed you would have picked up on it."

"What if I just hide away and not show...Lonnie wouldn't have a chance...."

"Exactly, and they wouldn't flush him out. The threat would always be there. No, Kitten, we have to go with this. You're the target...I hate having you at risk–make that devastated–but as I said...at least you have protection...but if he were to find you alone...."

"So you think he's the one stalking the neighbourhood?"

"No question...in his deceased mother's Volvo. He followed Ian the other day...may have thought it was you since the car came from here. The undercover boys are stalking him...they watch him while he watches our place...followed him when he followed Ian...saw what happened to him and just left him there. They don't want to pick him up until they have an air-tight case...they don't want to repeat this."

"So his dad knows about this?"

"Apparently. He's at least in touch with Brighton. They wouldn't tell me more than that."

"So they don't know what he intends to do to me?"

"I suspect they have some ideas but they aren't sharing. They're certain he doesn't have a gun. His dad says he wouldn't know how to use one. I notice they make sure he can't sit near you...always fill up anything adjacent."

"I'm not good at centre stage."

"Sorry, my love...if I could change that.... But it won't be forever. They're sure he'll act before we return to London. Let's hope so...and trust the Lord and all the protection He's placed around you."

"What about when we're not in the building...when we go to lunch...eat in the park? This is really scary."

"He followed us yesterday, but kept his distance, like he was just wondering what to do. I'm sure he was also followed but I couldn't spot anyone; guess...if they're good at undercover, I shouldn't be able to," he added.

"I feel like just staying here and studying for a while."

"Not a good idea."

"Why? Do you think he'd find us here?"

"He was here before we arrived, Lee. And his shadow...and the undercover boys. It's a cinch to find out when your classes are. Lonnie would know at least that much. His followers keep him in their sights. They all look different than they did yesterday. Don't look suddenly, but check out the ponytail...the one with the coffee and the book...the table behind the pillar there. Watch what he does when we get up to leave. The other one is behind us. My guess is that he'll stay and keep an eye on Lonnie."

Brett's movements were obvious signs they were leaving...picking up their juice bottles and putting them in recycle...helping Lee into her jacket...closing his briefcase...taking her backpack. She noticed that the ponytail had casually closed his book, yawned, deposited his coffee cup and sauntered toward the door a few paces ahead of them.

Pretty clever...doesn't give the impression of following anybody. I hope he's as good at protection as he is at deception.

Blast that wretched woman! And blast that gorilla...guards her like he's King Kong. Wonder whether she's staying all week...didn't expect this little operation to take this long...this could get exhausting. There they go again...maybe the parking lot would be the best.... He struggled to his feet, grabbed his backpack and fingered the pouch...yes, his weapon was ready...perhaps today would be the day.... His musings came to a crashing halt as his backpack caught the water glass and sent its contents flying...his clumsy attempt to grab the glass toppled the small table into the path of a passing debutante. Water splashed over her sweater and jeans; she screamed as she stumbled into the man beside her.

"Watch what you're doin' there mate," the man growled, as he set the table back on its legs.

Lonnie suddenly felt faint. He missed the chair and it skidded and toppled as he fell heavily backward. His last memory was of the wig flying off, and a female voice exclaiming, "Why it's Professor Hencken!"

CHAPTER FORTY-THREE

"Isn't this a bit strange?" she whispered as they resumed their studies at Bora Laskin. "No Lonnie, no *extra students*! Even the *pony tail* disappeared after his cell phone rang."

"Unusual is right. I wonder if they've picked up Lonnie. I'll call and find out before we go for lunch. Want to pick up a salad at Wendy's and picnic?"

"Sounds wonderful!"

"What a perfectly delightful day for a picnic!" she exclaimed. Then turning her attention to the small squirrel waiting for a handout, she added, "And don't you just love all these little squirrels...the way they seem to just fly through the trees!"

He nodded and smiled, obviously enjoying his wife as she enjoyed the freedom to relax and be herself.

"Are you going to tell me why we have no escorts?"

"Apparently Lonnie collapsed in the student lounge and they took him to the hospital."

"Oh, my! Did they say who took him?"

"I think the *shadow* and the other undercover agent. He caused quite a stir...apparently fainted...sounds like he upset a table and whatnot...guess somebody recognized him."

"You're kidding! That would have been something to see! I think he's a really sick man."

The squirrel decided to push his request and landed effortlessly on the table. Leanne offered the dried noodles from her salad. He picked one up in his small hand and looked it over.

"He'd really like those sliced almonds," Brett advised.

"Not a chance. *I can eat those*...he can have the noodles or starve," she chuckled.

She continued as though the squirrel had not interrupted, "He seems to look more peaked...more pale every day. What do you think might be wrong with him?"

"Well, he has had a lot of shock treatments...or it could be cancer.... I agree he looks terrible. I'm surprised that someone recognized him, especially in that get up!"

"Do you think the police will pick him up?"

"Apparently not. I talked to the inspector...they'll wait him out. They want some hard evidence. Meantime, we're free to enjoy our time here. Course it means he'll still be there when we return next month."

"Eeich," she made a face. Guess we'll deal with that when the time comes. Sure wish I knew what he intends to do...it might make it easier."

"If he really is that ill...and he intends to get you...he'll be frantic. Every delay will throw him into convulsions. Now he'll have to wait a whole month."

"So will we."

"Yes...so will we...and every month will be harder for you. I wish he'd just get on with it."

"Do you think his dad would give us any information? any insights?

"I've been wondering the same thing, though I can't imagine him letting down his guard–his pride will be a factor. Better leave it alone. We'll know soon enough."

"Well...."

"Well, what? What are you thinking?"

"I'm wondering if I should stay an extra week now, while he's sick, instead of coming back at the end of next month. I could get a lot of info for my new classes, and...."

He was quiet for so long, she wondered if he was on the same page, then, "I see a few problems with that, Kitten. We have only one car here...course I could catch a bus, or...you could drive me home. No, I guess I wouldn't like you out on the 401 by yourself in your condition...."

"What condition is that...do you mean *pregnant*?"

He ducked as though expecting a blow.

"Pregnancy is not a disease, Brett Walker! Quit treating me like an invalid!"

"Please don't call me, *Brett Walker*...especially in that tone. I might be a little protective, but...."

"A little?"

"Okay, okay. I could take the bus, but we still don't know how long he'll be in hospital, or incapacitated at home. I'm not about to leave my wife at the mercy of a maniac."

"Do you think there's any way we could find out about him...how sick he is...how long he might be in hospital?"

"His dad may know...but we're back to square one."

"What about the police?

"They're very protective of their information. You'd think we were the enemy."

"But–just listen to this–wouldn't we know he had been discharged when our *extra students* show up in the study hall?"

"I hoped you wouldn't think of that," he muttered.

She chuckled. "Or...what if I called the hospital every day and asked if he was allowed visitors? They'd let me know if he was still there."

"I can't imagine leaving you here, and going home, Lee."

"Well...it he's released from hospital, I'll call you at once. If you aren't free to come, I'll just head home."

"Please don't ask me to do this,Lee. I can't bear to leave you here. There's no point in my going home...I wouldn't accomplish a thing," he looked down, but not before she saw the stress...albeit fear...in his eyes.

"All right, Brett Walker," she said softly, "all right, Sweetheart, we'll do it your way."

He fought the huge restraining belt that kept him in the bed...the smaller ones that immobilized his arms...and the oxygen mask that covered his face and muffled his screams. His legs thrashed wildly as he tried to get the attention of a nurse...an orderly...anybody!

Having exhausted his small strength, he lay sweating...swearing. Obviously, he was in a hospital of some sort...getting a blood transfusion–as if he hadn't had enough of those! Another wretched nightmare! That must be it! He cursed as he struggled to shake it off.

As his mind began to focus, he wondered who had brought him here...and given permission for the blood. Time for that later...meantime...he needed out of here...*now!*

He trembled with rage as he struggled to reach the call button. The restraining device held fast...no amount of profanity persuaded it otherwise. He had to get out of here...he had only two days left and she would be gone!

CHAPTER FORTY-FOUR

"I almost hate to leave," she commented as they finished packing the car, "it's been such an enjoyable experience these last few days."

"Lonnie-less!" he commented with a smile. "Maybe we needed to experience the stress of having him around...in order to appreciate what we had–a peaceful environment for study... freedom to roam without fear...."

"How right you are, my love!"

"I have to admit I'll be glad when you're done. Even without Lonnie, it's a pretty stressful time...having you driving in...away from home...long hours of class work...study."

"That sounds torturous...and here I was enjoying the whole scene when I could have been bathing in self-pity!" she grinned.

"You are a rascal, Leanne Walker!"

Her grin continued, "I'm learning...tutored by an expert!"

The conversation resumed as they joined the late afternoon traffic. "Sure glad to hear that Uncle Ben is getting on so well. Aunt Maude was just bubbling when I talked to her last night. Guess they've even been out to the seniors' social. The way they enjoy each other just makes my heart smile."

"Mine, too. Ben is a dear saint of a man...he taught me a great deal...about life as well as Law. I'm glad he made it...for Maude...and for all of us."

"When is he going in for those tests? Didn't Maude say something about that?"

"Yeah, she did. But it didn't sound definite. With his quick recovery, they may just wait and see."

"Guess we owe him one for getting us together–initially when he suggested I work for you, and again when he advised me to article with you–though I doubt he would admit to that one. He's a character. I'm glad they're so thrilled about our baby."

"You know, Kitten, in light of the stroke, I'm wondering if we should tell them that we intend to call our baby, *Benjamin*." She nodded as he continued, "In the event that he has another and doesn't make it...well...I guess...I'm thinking Aunt Maude would appreciate the fact that he knew...and was looking forward to having a namesake."

"Yes...yes...a great idea! Let's have them for supper...and Dave and Sherry and Mandy... and then we'll tell them all at once. I can just see Mandy...she'll rename her dolls and make them into boys."

"I think we need to include Bob and his mom and dad."

"Good thought! And we'll need to ask them–the senior Wilsons, I mean–and Ben and Maude if they will be our adopted grandparents...since our wee one won't have any. What do you think?"

"I'd love it...they would, too."

"And what about your brother James? Uncle James...cute, huh?"

He smiled and nodded. "Maybe we should count before we add any more."

They planned as they drove...anticipating the joy the evening would bring to Ben and Maude and Dave's family.

CHAPTER FORTY-FIVE

"Rhonda called this morning," she commented as they enjoyed coffee in the lunch room. He looked questioningly at her as she continued, "I guess she and Brandy have hit it off. Looks like charges will be coming down the pike as we speak. I wonder if her dad knows...or even suspects...."

"Wow! Poor man won't know what hit him. He'll be destroyed."

"I don't mean to be crass...but it just might be his turn."

"You may well be right, but do you think she's doing the right thing...going about it like this, I mean?"

"Got any suggestions?"

"Not really."

"But you do think something needs to be done?"

"He needs to be stopped, if he's as bad as she says he is."

"I guess we'll know once it hits the press. My guess is there'll be another free-for-all like the Hencken thing...women coming out of the woodwork to accuse him."

"How is Rhonda feeling about all of this? Is she gloating or...?"

"Not at all; she was quite teary...fearful...feeling sorry for him...for herself...for the dozens of other young girls and women. A great deal of anguish."

"I'm pleased to hear that; she's making progress. My faith was not great that it could ever happen."

"I know what you mean. For a while, I wondered if she was real...or just getting better at the acting," she chuckled.

"I do feel for her, you know."

"No. I don't know. Why the turn about?"

"Not really a turn about. I share her pain, because of my own...we're both abused kids...but I didn't appreciate the way she went about getting even."

"You mean her antipathy for lawyers? Didn't you...uh...well...?" He glanced at her as she hesitated.

"Uh...well...what?"

"Didn't you...I mean...after your encounter with Tony and his mom...didn't you have similar feelings toward anyone with a Latin face?"

"Any chance you might wipe that off your hard drive?" he grinned and squeezed her fingers as he rose to go.

"Consider it done!" she smiled and blew him a kiss.

"Wow! Barbequed chicken and ribs! What a feast! Is this Walker style?" James grinned as he helped himself from the steaming platter.

"You bet...Brett style!" Leanne answered her brother in law.

"Looks like I could learn a few things from big brother," he smiled.

"Such as?" Dave prompted.

"His recipe for chicken and ribs...his recipe for finding a lovely lady and making her...."

He blushed as laughter erupted; clearly they thought he was going to say *pregnant.*. "Let me finish," he continued. "I was going to say *and making her his own.*"

Good natured joshing continued as the extended family enjoyed each other and the enormous meal set before them.

"So it's going to be a boy!" Uncle Ben beamed.

"Oh, yes, a boy...we're so delighted....just delighted!" Aunt Maude could hardly control herself. "A little boy! Oh, my! A playmate for Mandy...won't they be cute together!! What will you call him, dear?" She looked at Lee. "Has that been decided?"

Lee exchanged a look with Brett. "We're happy to tell you that it has," he answered for her.

Lee continued where he left off. "Yes, it took us a while...we both have family who are near and dear to us...whom we hope will have a part in his life...and whose names we would enjoy passing on to our son. Of course, we had to have a name that we just love since for the first few years we'll be using it dozens of times a day...." She smiled as they chuckled. "I wanted him named after his daddy, but Brett didn't think he could handle hearing me say, *No Brett*, over and over in ever-increasing volume." She looked for him to continue.

"So, when it came right down to the wire, we decided his second name would be after me, and the first would be after two people we both love and admire, Lee's father and Uncle Ben. We've decided on *Benjamin Brett*."

The split second silence was broken as Bob rose to his feet...others joined him quickly as joyous applause erupted. A tearful Uncle Ben struggled to his feet with Aunt Maude on one side and James on the other. He motioned but remained speechless.

"We're speechless...just speechless," his wife squealed, "What an honour! What an honour! Did you hear that, dear? A little grandson...named after you.... Oh my! Oh my! Did you ever? We're speechless...just speechless!" she continued, oblivious to the chuckles around her.

The elderly gentleman sat down heavily, wiping his tears. "I have never had a greater honour bestowed on me...not in all of my 75 years. A wee lad named after me! Thank you...thank you. I shall look forward..." his voice broke.

Dave wiped his own tears as he prayed silently that Uncle Ben might live to enjoy the wee lad who would bear his name.

CHAPTER FORTY-SIX

"Was that the inspector who called?" she asked since the information was not forthcoming.

"You don't miss much."

She smiled. "So?"

"Lonnie is out of hospital and recuperating at home. Inspector Brighton would like to chat...at his office when we arrive next week. Guess that means we should go in early Sunday evening."

"Any indication what he has in mind?"

"None except the obvious."

"I'm hoping the threat is removed...with Lonnie being sick. He sure doesn't look good at all...you know..." She stopped and looked at her husband. "You know what I think?"

"Better tell me...I could be here all day. I assume you've decided he has something terminal...AIDS, or something equally sinister."

Her mouth dropped open. "You really do read my mind, Brett Walker. That's exactly what I think. Why didn't I see it sooner?"

"See what?"

"AIDS."

They sat in silence...stunned that it hadn't occurred to them sooner. "He certainly looks like he has AIDS...the symptoms are overwhelming," he agreed. "Of course cancer is pretty debilitating, too."

"I can hardly consider such a thing! Think of the ramifications if he has AIDS...all those young women...and some guys, too, I understand."

"We'll need to find out, Lee. If he's dying of AIDS everyone deserves to know. And if he's known all along–and I'm sure he must have–he must be held accountable."

"I'm not sure what that means anymore. The man has raped– destroyed–dozens of young lives, and now he's out prowling–make that stalking–the university campus!"

"I agree, Kitten, but it can't go on. I wonder if they're still planning to appeal. Haven't heard anything about it lately. If Brighton isn't forthcoming with the information, I'll get in touch with Gil Hencken."

A brief knock and Melva walked in. "Have you seen the morning paper?" the secretary asked, her face a chalky white. She spread it quickly between them. "I can't believe it...honestly...I had no idea!"

"PROMINENT LAWYER CHARGED WITH SEXUAL ASSAULT," the paper bellowed; then sub-titled, "Twenty-seven Women Press Charges."

The lawyers looked at each other, then at the half-page, full-colour photo of Charles Fleming, resplendent in his well-known imported British tweeds...and handcuffs.

"How awful," from Leanne. "Do they really have to make a circus out of everything?"

"So now you're feeling sorry for him?"

"Aren't you? Seems that somewhere along the line his conscience must have been left behind...a veritable sociopath. What could he possibly have in life that has any meaning? And what's left to look forward to?"

"Right on all counts. But, considering the trail of chaos he's left behind...guess it's time to face the music. Do you think the twenty-seven women are those Rhonda knew about and got signatures for or....?"

She nodded. "She said it was only the beginning. She's sure that dozens more will get on the bandwagon once it starts to roll. If the Hencken thing is any indication, she's probably right."

CHAPTER FORTY-SEVEN

"Lonnie is very sick," Brett commented as they headed into Toronto. Brighton feels he would like to get even with you before he...."

"Oh, my! How destitute can a soul be...facing eternity...his only goal to get even? You know what I mean? I'd think he'd be a little concerned...spend a little time preparing to meet his Maker." He nodded as she continued, "So why does the inspector think this? Does he have any further ideas as to what he intends?"

"I'm asking myself those questions. He must have gotten some information from Gil Hencken. Course, he won't divulge anything. Just wanted us to *be alert to any probability,* as he put it.

They were both surprised to find Gil Hencken already seated in the inspector's sparsely furnished office. He rose and extended his hand, while the inspector indicated the chairs near the desk.

"I'm sure you must be surprised to find me here," Hencken began, then paused and cleared his throat.

"Mr. Hencken has been wanting to have a word with you," the inspector interjected, "and after some serious consideration, I felt something might be gained from the four of us discussing this together."

"Glad to have you join us," Brett addressed Gil Hencken, while Leanne looked on with astonishment.

"I...uh...I...that is...." the elderly lawyer began, his face reddening and sweat standing out on his forehead. "I have been meaning to get in touch. There...uh...there are some things that I think you need to know about my son."

Leanne looked from Hencken to Brighton to her husband. When no one spoke, she suggested, "Please continue Mr. Hencken."

Encouraged by her charitable tone, he added, "My son is gravely ill. I just dropped him at the hospital...at University Hospital...on my way here. I don't know if they will be admitting him...I assume so...but he wouldn't let me come in with him...he is very independent...." His voice trailed off as he looked from Leanne to Brett, and mopped his brow with a man-size tissue. "Might I have a glass of water?"

"By all means," the inspector buzzed his secretary. "And we do have some fresh coffee on the way; Julie will be right along."

"Do you know the nature of Lonnie's illness?" Brett's question was pointed and the senior lawyer squirmed under his gaze.

"Well, I'm not sure how relevant that is right at this time...I know my son didn't actually have a relationship with your wife...." Hencken hedged.

"Now, Gil," the inspector began. "We both know that you can speak more plainly than that. We also know that this will be public knowledge before the week is out. I suggest you come clean...you owe it to this couple to tell them what you told me on Friday."

The silence was deafening as Lonnie's father attempted to gain composure, and save face while knowing it was an impossible task.

"Yes...yes...I suppose so."

Leanne couldn't help but compare the self-assured, arrogant Hencken at Lonnie's bail hearing with the pitiful one who sat before her now. *He looks so old...defeated...used up,* she decided. When he failed to go on, she asked, "Mr. Hencken, does Lonnie have AIDS?" She watched him dart a quick glance at the inspector before he nodded.

"You were right, Graham." Then turning to Leanne and Brett, "Graham thought you would probably have figured it out by now. I don't think anyone else knows, but, yes, we must make it public...he has done a great deal of damage...." His voice broke and Leanne touched his arm with a comforting gesture.

"I know I owe you an apology...I'm sorry I didn't know about the illness when we applied for bail...of course we won't be pursuing the appeal," he added, then continued. "Lonnie was so desperate to be out of the hospital–jail, he called it–and I was more than happy to believe the psychiatrists...that his behaviour was caused by the chemical imbalance. I just wanted the nightmare to end." He paused as Julie arrived and served the coffee.

She smiled and filled a water glass from the pitcher on her tray.

"Tell them what you told me, Gil. Tell them the real reason he was so desperate to get out."

The elderly lawyer nodded. "Yes...yes...of course...but I need to back up...perhaps if you have a little background.... I have to admit to not knowing my son very well; he was very close with his mother. I guess I'm getting a little ahead of myself. My wife and I were both professional people, and we married a little later than most folk. We were...how shall I say? We were a little beyond the ideal age for child-bearing and Loretta wanted a child...very badly. After a few years of marriage, I agreed to adopt, and several years later our little boy arrived.

"From the beginning...how shall I say this? From the moment we got Lonnie...he belonged to his mother. She simply took him over and would allow no suggestions as to his care, his education, his extra curricular activities, his social life. Loretta became a different person...a stranger to me...nor would she allow me to father the child. I watched from the sidelines with a great feeling of unease...despairing for his future. He was spoiled...indulged beyond reason ...nothing was denied him that money could buy. His quick mind found ways to manipulate the system and his mother and I, his friends, his teachers. My efforts to intervene...to reason with his mother were met with hostility."

"Let me get that for you, Mr. Hencken," Leanne rose quickly to refill the water glass and placed it in his trembling hand. He reached for another tissue and wiped the droplets that stood out on his forehead and trickled down the sides of his now florid face. *Oh, God, help! I think he's going to have a stroke.*

"A little more coffee?" Graham Brighton picked up the carafe and offered refills as he waited for his old friend to regain his composure.

"That must have been very difficult for you, Mr. Hencken," Leanne offered.

He nodded slowly, then began again, "In my naivete...stupidity...I hoped he might grow out of his extreme self-centeredness. It never happened; he became totally self-absorbed. As a teen, he felt he had the right to as many little girls...." He paused...closed his eyes as the tears came, then continued. "Of course his mother took care of the damage...she simply paid his way out of the scrapes. Wealth is not always a blessing," he added in a hoarse whisper.

"It was never enough. When I realized the extent to which he had manipulated his mother's finances, I took steps to protect her from him...from herself. He was furious when he found out she no longer had unlimited access. He turned on her...extracted a promise she would force my compliance. She tried everything. She was hysterical...beyond reason...accused me of driving him away from her. She would not admit that the bruises on her face and arms were Lonnie's handiwork.

"Loretta passed away four years ago," he paused as Brett and Leanne looked at him with both sympathy and expectancy.

"They said it was a heart attack," he continued. "But I know it was caused by a broken heart. She had put her life into Lonnie, and far from appreciating her...he was furious that the goose had quit laying golden eggs. He didn't speak to me until his finances ran out. I helped him from time to time...for his mother's sake, of course...though he found it very hard to be civil. He simply wanted control of our assets...bank accounts. There was no reason why he couldn't live within his means...he had a good education...a very expensive one, I might add.

"I have to admit that I really had no idea of the scope of his transgressions...not until the media...." he dropped his head in his hands and sobbed. "I have never felt my own failure so deeply, as I did that morning...*The Star* arrived on my doorstep with the pictures....

"I'm a little late, Mrs. Walker, but would you still accept my apology on behalf of my son?"

Leanne looked at him questioningly, but she was too shocked to respond. She glanced at Brett and noted his face livid with rage. *Apology, indeed!*

The senior Hencken waited, looking from one to the other. "I hoped you would understand that I did what I could when I found out about his intentions toward you. I came to Inspector Brighton," he glanced at the inspector who nodded in agreement. "I...we believe that he might still like to do you harm...."

"Perhaps you could tell them why you think so?" the inspector interjected.

"Well...yes...he is so very angry at being thwarted...exposed...."

His lengthy pause gave Brett opportunity, "Do you know what kind of harm he is planning? Can you enlighten us?"

"I don't think it's really relevant...not any more...he's really too ill...though he would harm Leanne if he could."

"Tell them, Gil. Tell them what you told me."

"Well, yes...I suppose I must. I came upon Lonnie in his room filling a needle with his own blood. I had found one in the car a few weeks earlier. He assured me it was to be dropped off at the hospital...that he didn't have time to go in and wait for a test."

Again he paused, and the inspector explained, "We had the blood tested the first time Gil brought it in, to make sure it was Lonnie's. The lab turned up AIDS. We put two and two together when we found out he was invading the law library with a loaded needle in his backpack."

The blood drained from Leanne's face. "He was going to give me AIDS! HE WAS GOING TO GIVE ME AIDS,! she shreiked.

Brett sat silently...his face white with shock. Controlling his anger with extreme effort, he turned on the two men, "And you both knew this? And you put my wife...and child...at risk?"

"Hold on, hold on," the inspector interjected. "We knew he had AIDS, and we knew he was at the library, but the contents of the backpack only became known when he collapsed in the student lounge. One of my men helped deliver him to the hospital."

Brett continued to look him in the eye, his anger scarcely under control.

"I understand your feelings here, Brett. As I explained last time you were in, we needed to have something concrete to charge him with...to put him away. Carrying a needle in your backpack is not against the law...not until we know the intent. If we pick him up on breach of parole, he'll be out again before long. We provided as much security for your wife as we could. I understand they even escorted her to the bathroom."

"Indeed!" from an indignant Leanne.

The look on Brett's face was uncompromising. "So what do you plan to do now?"

"I really don't think he's a threat," his father began. "He's just too ill to harm anyone... he's back at the hospital...."

"We're keeping up our vigil," the inspector interrupted. "My boys won't leave the hospital until he does." Noting the exasperated look on Brett's face, he added, "And we're still providing a cover for Leanne...as long as you're within city limits...."

"Are you okay, Kitten?" her husband asked as they drove toward the university. "You look all in. Do you think you should be going to class?"

"I'm not feeling the greatest; it won't be the best day of my life, but with Lonnie out of the way–at least for the moment–it's got to be better than some we've been through."

"Good thing you have reserved parking," he commented as he swung into the full lot. The non-descript vehicle behind him did not escape his notice. *Wonder where they think they'll find a space.*

"I'd best hustle...I don't want to miss another class this morning."

"Let me get that for you," he grabbed his brief case and hurried to open her door.

She struggled to her feet, then suddenly shrieked, "Brett! Behind you....!"

He whirled as the madman lunged ...arm poised to strike. With split-second timing Brett stepped in front of his wife, using his briefcase as a shield. The loaded needle flew through the air as Lonnie hit the ground beneath the weight of two pseudo law students. Obscenities polluted the air.

"Brett," she cried, her eyes wide with terror. "Are you okay? Did he get you?"

"Almost," he tried a grin and held up his briefcase with the embedded needle. "Guess my briefcase will have AIDS." His joke fell flat as Leanne turned white and leaned against the car.

"Are you both all right?" The officer turned from placing a hand-cuffed, screaming Lonnie in one of the police vehicles that had seemingly appeared from nowhere.

Brett held up the briefcase. "Looks like it took the rap for both of us," he commented. "He nearly got Leanne." He glanced at her, then quickly opened the car door and eased her in. "I'd best get her to the hospital...I thinks she's in shock."

"I guess we haven't been formally introduced. I'm Detective Dan Klassen," he held out his hand.

"Good to meet you, Detective," the lawyer grinned and accepted the handshake, "and thanks for your help. Guess I wasn't sure...."

"If we were still on the job?" He chuckled, realizing how he must look to Brett–the long hair, the stud in his ear, the sweatshirt and jeans. "We've had our Lonnie under surveillance since he left the house this morning. The trip to the hospital was a ploy to get his father off his back. He just grabbed a cab and headed over here. He's been hiding out...waiting for your arrival. Good thing he's as weak as he is...I'll let the squad car take him in and we'll escort you to the hospital. He'll need to go there, too, once we've booked him. Don't worry," he chuckled at Brett's frown, "we're still on the job."

CHAPTER FORTY-EIGHT

"Home just feels so–o-o good," Leanne exclaimed as her husband switched off the newscast, and she laid back on the recliner. "I mean...it's always good, but after that week in Toronto.... Honestly, hon, It just couldn't end too soon for me!"

Brett nodded, his mind lingering on the latest news report on Lonnie Hencken. "How do you feel about this latest development, Lee?"

She gave him an enquiring look? "Which development is that?"

"You know...the documentary that reporter is working on. What's his name? Bates? Yes, I think it's Bates. A documentary on Lonnie's life."

"Everybody wanting a piece of the pie...he could have had mine," she smiled. "Guess I wonder what slant he'll put on it...whether Gil Hencken will be consulted, or whether he'll try to put an end to further publicity. Guess it's a bit late for that."

"What about you? They're pretty determined to coerce you...."

"Well, they tried before. This documentary has been in the works for some time. I was of the impression that Lonnie was fueling it from the psychiatric hospital...making himself the victim of jealous rivals at the university."

"You're right. That was in the works. But it's way too late to play the victim...with all these latest developments. Your involvement will certainly be necessary if they want the facts."

"I don't plan to be interviewed...unless of course you have some compelling reason...."

He raised his eyebrow in surprise. "None! I was hoping you'd decline. But, tell me what you're thinking."

"The media has been there whenever Lonnie was arrested–twice at my place, and now in the parking lot. They were at his hearings, his release from the psych hospital...they just materialize out of the pavement. Why would I want to go through it all...all over again? And why would I want my picture smeared all over the front page, the TV news, and on and on? When people recognize me on the street, I don't want it to be for that reason."

"Very well put, my love. Guess we better take steps to stop the harassment. You know that two of the messages on voice mail are offering to buy your story."

"So, let's cancel voice mail until the storm blows over."

"Good idea. And we'll need to ensure they don't lie in wait at the office."

"What do you suggest?"

"I'm not sure. They'll probably follow us when we leave home. Maybe we could get you a disguise...borrow something from Uncle Ben or Aunt Maude. Why don't we go there for an evening, borrow his car and leave for a hotel, or to Dave's? If they think it's Ben...or Maude... they may just wait for us at their house."

"So...I'll show up at the office looking like Uncle Ben?" she chuckled.

"No. Well...maybe. You'd be in Ben's car...Ben's clothes. Change when you get there. Or...what about a blonde wig? They'd think you were Sherry."

"Honestly, Brett! I was never any good at camouflage...charades. Can you just imagine the reaction when the secretaries see me!"

"They'll love it."

"What if I just change my office hours...come at a different time...by myself...or with Dave rather than you?"

"All of that will be helpful, but they hang around all day. You'll have to be creative...elude them, I'm afraid."

"Ah! What price fame!" she grinned.

They both reacted as the door bell rang. "Not another one! Why don't you just stay put and I'll deal with it?"

She nodded and he headed to the door. The exchange was abrupt, and an indignant Brett returned to the family room. "They're setting up tripods on the lawn."

"So...we'll take the BMW whenever we go out. With the darkened windows, they'll never see me in the back seat. Thank the Lord for an attached garage."

He picked up the cordless phone and made arrangements with Uncle Ben. They would be delighted to have them call, and yes there would be room to park in the garage so Leanne could exit undetected.

"My dears, I don't know why you shouldn't just stay here for a few days until the heat is off. We'd love to have them, wouldn't we Ben?"

He nodded, smiling. "Of course, of course, we would. Why not use one of our vehicles to come and go?"

"Would either of you want to trade for a purple Lexus for a few days?" Brett chuckled at the thought of Ben behind the wheel.

"Love to...love to! I've been wanting to try that Lexus. Maude has been after me.... Good time to try it out...eh, Maude?"

"Yes, dear...I would say so!" She winked conspiratorially at Leanne.

"We are concerned for you folk. You know some of the reporters followed us over here and are waiting down the block. I'm sure they don't know that Lee is with me. She laid low in the back seat, and the windows are darkened. Now they're at both places...waiting for a chance to pounce. How do you feel about...?"

"I don't think it should worry us. What do you think Maude?"

"We'll be fine. Especially if they just wait down the block. I doubt they'll follow us around like they do Leanne." Turning to Leanne, she continued, "You poor dear...how will you get around with them after you?" Then, as her thoughts progressed, she added, "And how will you be able to get to work? Go to church? Oh, my dear!"

"Well, I thought she should borrow some clothes from Uncle Ben," Brett chuckled.

"Not a bad idea; not bad at all." Ben offered.

"Yes...yes...he has lots to spare. He's lost so much weight, you know...two full sizes."

"Starting to look pretty trim, there, Uncle Ben," Brett encouraged. "So what occasioned the weight loss...?"

"Well the doctor has been after us for years...wanted us to join the *Walk for your Life* program, but Ben just wasn't interested. I was afraid he was getting too heavy but he was busy with other things...," she broke off and looked at Ben. "Why don't you tell them, dear."

"Yes, well, I always intended to do something about it, but then the little stroke was a wake-up call...and...and...I found out I was going to be grandpa...and...well, I knew I needed to adopt a healthier lifestyle! Besides I was having a hard time tying my shoes...how could I play on the floor with Benjie?" he grinned self-consciously.

"Oh, Uncle Ben–guess I'd better make that *Grandpa Ben*–its so special to hear you say that! And yes—you'll need to play marbles and set up toy trains," she smiled.

"We're just loving the Lexus, dear!" Aunt Maude bubbled. "Did you get to the office safely this morning?"

"We did! Another successful camouflage. The staff are having fits. Even Dave didn't recognize me this morning. I wore the blonde wig that Sherrie picked up for me. Yesterday I tucked my hair under a scarf, and added Uncle Ben's old hat and suit coat. I looked rather like a bag lady."

"My dear, my dear!" the older lady chuckled, "and you didn't think charades was your thing!" she added.

"I do have a problem now, Aunt Maude...Brett likes me better as a blonde."

"Don't believe a word of it...Aunt Maude...she's gorgeous whatever she wears...even when she's a bag lady," Brett cut in.

"Now, now, you two, you just take care of each other, and keep those reporters at bay," she added as an afterthought.

"So...tell me what you're enjoying about the Lexus," Brett asked.

"All of it, dear, it's just a special little car...I love the interior...the comfort...the gadgets...the sun roof...the color...but most of all I'm enjoying the attention I get when I drive it. Really, at my age...you know...at my age we don't get that any more...to say nothing of being tailed by the media," she giggled. "Are you interested in selling it, dear?" she added, tongue in cheek.

"It's time for lunch, Kitten. I've asked the staff to join us today." Brett grinned in the doorway.

"If I didn't know better, I'd say I'm smelling Chinese food," she said as she followed him to the lunch room. "Well...I'll be!! Where did all this come from?" she indicated the many cartons on the table.

"Uncle Ben called. He doesn't think sandwiches and quick lunches all week are healthy for little Ben...he ordered *proper food*. Look at that almond diced chicken...ribs...and those vegetables! Look at this..." He read the note, "*No flour in almond chicken, and fried rice.*"

"My word! He certainly takes his grand parenting seriously," Dave grinned. "Glad he's looking after *Uncle*, too."

"You are looking stressed, Lee," her husband reached across the desk and took her hand. "Is this cat-and-mouse with the media getting to you?"

She shook her head. "Have you seen this?" she shoved over The Star with yet another picture of Lonnie splashed on the front. "He looks so awful, Brett. Shouldn't we be trying to...?"

She paused at the look on his face, then continued, "Well, I mean...he looks so hopeless."

"What do you have in mind?" he ventured at length.

"Someone should care about him...enough to visit...to counsel...."

"Leanne," his voice had that stern, no-nonsense tone, "*you* are not going to see him," he leaned across the desk to better make his point.

"What about you?" she asked shrugging her shoulders slightly.

"So what would you like me to do...kill him?"

"Brett Walker!"

He chuckled. "Then don't send me."

"Actually...I was really wondering about Paul Hayes...or maybe Pastor Bill Somerville."

"Hayes is a professional psychologist. Lonnie already has psychiatrists running after him...it would hardly be ethical...."

"You're right, of course. I didn't think of that. What about Bill?"

"We could discuss it with him, of course, but the case is so high profile.... There's always the chance his reputation might be compromised. Some cub reporter deciding he's looking for media attention...guess we've been down that road a time or two. But, we'll look into it."

CHAPTER FORTY-NINE

The Star learned today of the untimely death.... Leanne looked up into the stricken face of her secretary. The women stared speechlessly at one another.

"Does Brett...?"

Melva shook her head. "I just saw it," her voice a hoarse whisper. "Ask him to come in?"

The secretary knocked on his door, then opened it slowly.

"Yes, Melva."

She attempted to speak...then wordlessly beckoned him.

"Are you okay?" he rose quickly.

She shook her head as she exited, leaving the door ajar.

"Leanne...Kitten...you're white as a ghost."

She handed him the paper and watched as he read the article.

"So...Lonnie is gone. An untimely death...sounds like suicide...."

His wife nodded.

"Why don't I just call Inspector Brighton. If anybody knows about this, he will."

The exchange was brief. Leanne looked questioningly at him as he sat in stunned silence.

"Tell me," the whispered.

"Yes, it was suicide."

"In the hospital?"

He nodded.

"How could he possibly...in there, I mean?"

"Don't ask, Lee. You don't want to know?"

Her breath caught in her throat. "A needle?"

The look on his face said it was true. "Oh, God!" she moaned. "Oh, God, no!"

211

CHAPTER FIFTY

"Nine pounds...I can hardly believe it!" Sherrie exclaimed for the fourth time. "Honestly, Leanne...nine pounds!"

"Felt more like twenty," Leanne smiled at the gathering around her bed.

"It's my turn, dear. You've been monopolizing him. He needs to meet Grandma Maude."

"There, there, my love...all in good time! Benjie and Grandpa are only starting to get acquainted. Eh, Benjie?" Then looking at the tiny bundle in his arms, he added, "Now we'll just get you on home in a day or two, and get that train set put together," he winked at Brett.

"So this is Benjamin Brett Walker," his adopted Grandpa Wilson arrived on the scene. "What a little man! Looks like he favours his daddy."

"No doubt about that," from Uncle Dave. I can just see the shingle on the side of his crib–B. B. Walker. On second thought, maybe his second name should have been after our cousin, Martyn," he teased.

"Whatever for?"

"Think of the initials!"

The new father watched the bantering with a warm smile...his heart full. *Thank You, God,* he breathed. *Thank you for the family you made me a part of...and now our precious little guy. Give me an undivided heart, Lord...that I might lead him in Your ways.*

212

Printed in the United States
33641LVS00002B/262-426

9 781413 781090